BOOK 2 – ARIZONA

BEAUTIFUL DEAD

Eden Maguire

Hodder
Children's
Books

A division of Hachette Children's Books

Typeset in Berkeley Book by Avon DataSet Ltd,
Bidford on Avon, Warwickshire

Printed and bound in Great Britain by
CPI Bookmarque Ltd, Croydon, Surrey

The paper and board used in this paperback by Hodder Children's Books
are natural recyclable products made from wood grown in
sustainable forests. The manufacturing processes conform to the
environmental regulations of the country of origin.

Hodder Children's Books
a division of Hachette Children's Books
338 Euston Road, London NW1 3BH
An Hachette UK company
www.hachette.co.uk

For my two beautiful daughters

Phoenix Rohr changed me. He exploded into my life like a bright shooting star out of a big, dark sky and lit up my world. Before I met Phoenix I was a half-person – unfinished and scared. Afterwards, for a few short weeks, I was whole.

He and I did it for each other. We held together against the rough world, my hand in his, his arm around my shoulder.

The truth is, people in my world have a habit of losing their lives – four kids from our school in one year. It makes for intensity – every day you grasp what you've got and live it. Love and sex, sharing each moment. I held on to Phoenix like he was my saviour.

And then it shattered. I lost him – three small words. He was in a fight and he died.

I looked for him everywhere. I drove my car out of town through the shaking aspens and tall redwoods to where the jagged hills joined the sky. 'Phoenix.' I whispered it a thousand times. His name was all I had.

Phoenix – the fourth on a roll-call of students who would never return. One – two – three – four hits to the heart and the last one was the worst by a million miles. 'Phoenix.'

I clung to memories. His kisses, his touch – midsummer days when we swam in Deer Creek, evenings of him turning up the sound system in my car and driving us out to Hartmann Lake, me resting my head on his shoulder and trying to count the stars. For a time I was scared that I'd forget.

Then the wings of angels, ghosts, spirits in limbo – whatever you want to call them – began to beat. And Phoenix came back.

I don't want to talk with anyone. I need to be alone.

OK, so everything worked out for Jonas – and that was partly down to me. But I still hold the fate of three Beautiful Dead in my hands. It's true – I do. *Arizona, Summer and Phoenix. Arizona, Summer, Phoenix.* In that order – the names run in my head like a mantra.

'Darina, I wish you would stay home more. We could do stuff – have a pedicure, go shopping.' This is Laura, my mom.

'Darina, you have to quit driving the convertible. It eats gas.' My stepdad, Jim.

You get the picture.

'Meet us at the mall. Lucas and Christian will be there.' Jordan and Hannah. Chirpy-chirpy-cheep-cheep chickadees.

And Logan Lavelle. 'Darina, why don't you hang at my

place like we used to? I have a cool new DVD we can watch.'

Back off, all of you. Leave me alone. My body language ought to have done it, but these guys are too thick-skinned to read it. Or maybe they care about me.

I drive the car anyway, way out through Centennial, always in the same direction towards Foxton. Into the mountains, rising sheer on each side of the freeway, blocking out the blue sky.

I blast music into the quiet air. I put my foot on the gas.

Speed is the key to lifting the weight from my shoulders, leaving everyone behind. *Drive, baby, drive!* I'm in amongst the burn-out area. Miles of forest-fire have left black, twisted stumps, fallen trunks, grey earth. In ten years maybe green stuff will start to grow.

I'm out of the tree carnage, pushing higher into the mountains and the redwoods are green again against the pink rock, and I'm shedding my heavy secret, it's sliding from my shoulders because out here nobody can pressure me. I'm safe.

The beat of the music pounds my eardrums. Guitars whine. I yell the lyrics as I grip the steering wheel and lean forward in my seat. Lipgloss-red bodywork and creamy beige leather, with silver trim. Brandon Rohr showed expensive taste when he found me this car. I pass

Turkey Shoot Ridge, ten minutes from Foxton. Thirty minutes from the Beautiful Dead.

I guess I'm fixated. I *know* I am. Every moment, every breath I take, I long for Phoenix, his eyes reading what's in my head and heart, his arms around me. Why can't I be with him twenty-four seven, I want to know.

Here's Foxton – a straggle of wooden houses, a general store with boarded windows, a junction without a traffic sign. I take the side road, past the fishermen's cabins overlooking the racing water where Bob Jonson finally took revenge for Jonas's death – forced Matt Fortune off the track and they both smashed against the rocks and drowned. They took Matt's Harley back to Charlie Fortune and he fixed it up for himself to ride. I shudder when I think about that. *Don't* think about it, Darina. Drive on.

I'm clear of the houses and the track has turned to dirt. There's nothing beyond this point, so I need to get out of the car and go by foot along the path the mule deer have made when they head for the stand of aspens on the ridge. This is the fifth, maybe sixth time I've driven up here since Jonas left, and always I meet silence and emptiness. The wind blows through the aspens but there are no wings beating, no force field telling far-siders like me to back off.

Phoenix, it's me. Where are you? I need to see you. When he holds me in his arms my heart steadies. It's the only time I feel I'm home. *If I carry your secret much longer, I'll fall apart. Tell Hunter, tell the others, I can't do this alone.*

I climb to the ridge and I'm out of breath as I stand in the shade of the rusting water tower. You can look through the trees down into the next valley and never see the old barn. The aspen leaves shake and rustle – like wings? It's beautiful, really beautiful – the aspens and the sloping hillside, yellow spikes of Indian tobacco plant standing proud of the silvery meadow grass. And the big, big sky.

But no, I'm still not hearing the sound of beating wings – only the thump of my own heartbeat and the rasp of my breath, and I get no sense of Phoenix and the Beautiful Dead. I look for him as I stride down the slope, look so hard that maybe I miss the obvious and fail to spot his tall, still figure by the barn door, turned to me and waiting. He *will* be there, if wishing and longing can make it happen.

My legs swish through the grass. I crouch and crawl under the razor-wire fence. And I can see straight into the barn because the door is swinging open like always. 'Phoenix?' I say out loud as I step into the darkness. There's the dust smell in my nostrils and the stall partitions rotting and leaning at crazy angles. Ancient horse tack is hanging from hooks, cobwebs trail from rafter to rafter. 'Please!'

Let's get this straight. This is where the Beautiful Dead hang out. They don't let you see them unless they want to. In fact, they need to be secret, to keep out people from the far side – that's you and me – or else they're . . . I was about to say 'dead', but that would be weird. I mean, Phoenix, Hunter, Arizona, Summer and the rest are history already. They're *revenants*, come *back* from the dead.

The barn was empty – I checked every inch, even the hayloft, where narrow shafts of sunlight fell across the rotting floor. This was where I'd first glimpsed Phoenix, in the centre of a chanting circle – the Beautiful Dead and their overlord welcoming him back from limbo. *Bam!* – my mind exploded. By the time I gathered the pieces, my dead boyfriend was part of Hunter's gang and he had his death mark to prove it. An angel-wing tattoo between his shoulder blades, where the knife went through.

Phoenix, come back! I pleaded.

I left the barn and walked across the yard, hope draining from me. 'Hunter!' I yelled. 'This is you doing this. I hate you!'

The zombie overlord kept them invisible. He wasn't ready for me to see the Beautiful Dead again. He would take his time, let them gather their strength after the Jonas thing. And you should also know that they have no free will and Hunter rules every single thing they do. Even though he stayed invisible, he heard me saying I hated him, right there and then. That's another seriously useful superpower he has.

I decided to appeal to his softer side, though I knew he didn't have one.

'Hunter, please. I miss Phoenix. It hurts like hell.'

No answer as I stood by the flatbed of the rusty truck. *Still* no answer as I stepped on to the house porch and peered through the grimy window. I made out the rocking-chair by the kitchen range, the table covered in a hundred years of dust. I turned the handle and shoved with my shoulder against the locked door. 'Hunter, I hate you,' I murmured.

A month earlier I would have walked away and told myself that the whole zombie thing was crazy. It was what grief was doing to my fevered brain – making me see things that weren't there. I mean, how else do you cope when the person you love most in your life gets stabbed in a fight and dies? Loss doesn't cover that feeling. You need to cry and hit out at the same time, you fall down the deepest, darkest hole and the sides are smooth and there's nothing to cling on to. According to Kim Reiss, the therapist Laura sent me to see, this is when the brain is most likely to play cruel tricks.

But that was four weeks back. Since then, I'd time travelled and come up with the answer to the mystery of Jonas Jonson's death, and I was a true believer. So I knew Hunter the zombie overlord was definitely holding out on me and stopping me from seeing Phoenix. He was *choosing* to stay away.

'If you keep on like this, I won't come back,' I threatened. I sounded like a wuss, even to myself. 'You need me. I'm your link with the far side.'

Silence and space – nothing else.

'Arizona needs me,' I insisted. It was close to a year since she'd drowned in Hartmann Lake. 'Her time is starting to run out.'

The wind blew along the porch, lifting a loose board in the roof. I'd tried every trick I knew to make the Beautiful Dead come back, and all for nothing. Still I stayed for the whole morning, sitting in the cab of the ancient truck, staring up at Angel Rock.

Finally I climbed down. 'OK, you win,' I muttered, setting off up the hill. 'Anyhow, I have a funeral to go to.'

It wasn't Bob Jonson's actual funeral. After four in one year, I don't go any more. So I went along afterwards to the wake.

All the old bikers were there in their fringed leathers, with their goatee beards and their wild grey hair. The Harleys were parked in a half circle outside Bob's favourite bar. I was underage, so I hung out in the parking lot with Jordan, Lucas and Logan.

'This is too sad.' There were tears in Jordan's eyes. A lock of wavy dark hair fell over her face. I was waiting for shy-boy Lucas to put an arm around her shoulder and comfort her.

The guy didn't make a move so I stepped in and handed Jordan a Kleenex.

'You were there, Darina,' she said. 'You saw him ride over the cliff.'

I nodded. 'It wasn't an accident. Bob forced Matt to skid over the edge, then he revved his engine and rode after him. He definitely wanted it to end.'

'It's still too tragic,' Jordan insisted. 'The guy had his revenge. He didn't have to die.'

'Yes, he did.' Logan spoke, not looking at Jordan, but right at me. 'There was nothing else for Bob, not after Jonas was killed. Life was hollow. He was always at my place, drinking with my dad. I personally watched the guy fall apart. Right, Darina?'

I nodded again. 'Did Jonas's mom make the trip from Chicago?' I asked him.

'Yeah. She flew down with her sister. They're inside with the guys.'

'How did she look?' Jordan asked.

You can lose your son then split with your husband because he's crazy with grief, but you can still care. And the proof is – she came to the wake. 'How do you guess she would look?' I asked.

Other kids from Ellerton High were showing up. Someone turned up the CD player in his car and began blasting out Bob Dylan from way back. A track called 'Knock-knock-knocking on Heaven's Door'.

'Bob Jonson would be cool with this,' Logan said.

The bleak words to the songs made me want to cry but I'd handed Jordan my last Kleenex. Instead, I stared at the shiny metal tubes and tanks of the motorcycles and tried to remember how totally happy Jonas and Zoey had been.

'Why are you smiling?' Jordan asked impatiently. 'You're weird, Darina.' She walked away, with Lucas trailing behind.

'No, you're not,' Logan assured me, trying to stick a Band Aid on what he supposed would be my shredded ego. 'I know where you're coming from.'

I stared at him. 'You think you do, Logan, but you don't!'

There's back story here between me and Logan, which

means I push him away whenever he tries to get close. To be fair on myself though, he definitely trades on me knowing him since kindergarten, living on the next street and him buying me a white orchid corsage and taking me to our first prom – like we're always going to be that close, Disney bluebirds in the trees and wedding bells in the distance. Not!

I caught the hurt look in his eyes, the hand running uncertainly through his curly brown hair. Then he went into damage limitation. 'Well, no one knows exactly how another person is feeling – obviously. But no way are you weird.'

'Thanks,' I mumbled, spotting Zoey's mom dropping Zoey off in the parking lot. Zoey was still in a wheelchair, but her hair was styled and coloured and she was looking good. I went right across to talk with her.

'Hey,' she said softly.

I tried to pinpoint the way she smiled at me and scraped up the word 'wan'. I must have read it somewhere. 'Hey, Zoey,' I replied. She looked small and fragile in the wheelchair beside the monster Dynas and Softtails. 'I guess this is hard for you?'

She nodded. 'I came because of Jonas.'

'Have you still got his Harley buckle?' I asked. With Zoey, there was no ice to break. We just jumped right in to the stuff that mattered.

Raising her sweatshirt, she showed me that she was wearing it on her belt.

'What do you think, Darina – that Jonas and his dad are together now?'

'Big question!' I shrugged. 'It depends what you believe.'

There was a long silence. A couple of long-haired, badge-wearing, Bud-toting guys came out of the bar and sat astride their bikes. Two women wearing tailored black jackets and black trousers stood just inside the door. I recognized the fair, petite one as Jonas's mom.

'What do *you* believe?' Zoey wanted to know.

What did I do now? Did I shrug the question off, or did I give her what she wanted to hear? 'I guess they are,' I mumbled.

'Together,' she repeated with a sigh. 'You're not just saying that?'

I was side-stepping here. I knew for certain that Jonas had split from the group of Beautiful Dead the day his dad died – next stop freedom and peace for them both. That was the way Phoenix had explained it. But I couldn't breathe a word to Zoey. 'I believe it,' I said through clenched teeth.

Did you ever have a secret so big that it screamed to get out every time you opened your mouth? I pictured myself jumping up on to the saddle of one of the Harleys, stretching my arms wide and yelling, 'Listen to this, all of you! Jonas and his dad are cool. They're free. They got the peace they wanted. Be happy for them!'

'Darina – are you OK?' Zoey asked.

'I'm good,' I lied.

Luckily she moved on. 'There's Mrs Jonson. Shall I speak to her? What do you think, Darina?'

'I say yes. Do you want me to tell her hello, get her to come over here?'

Zoey shook her head. After multiple surgeries to fuse her spine in the places where it was broken in the Jonas crash, it was still an effort for her to raise herself out of her wheelchair and take slow, unsteady steps towards the door of the bar.

The kids in the parking lot did the decent thing and tried not to stare. One of the grey-haired bikers straddling his Dyna put down his beer, went up to her and said, 'Hey, let me help.' Together they went up the single step into the doorway.

Haley Jonson flinched when she saw Zoey, then set her face in a smile. 'Zoey, look at you!'

Zoey spread her hands like she'd performed a magic trick. 'Da-dah!'

'Hey, that's great,' Haley said, her voice choked, her

eyes filling up. She stared at Zoey for a long time, maybe thinking: *If someone had to survive the crash, why couldn't it have been my Jonas?* A dozen emotions fluttered across her pale face, then she took Zoey's hand. 'It's good to see you,' she whispered at last.

'Did you hear?' Zoey murmured. 'Darina finally helped me remember exactly what happened.'

'Honey, stop!'

Zoey dropped her gaze.

It was like everyone in the bar and the parking lot was holding their breath, waiting for a break in the unbearable tension between Jonas's mother and his girlfriend.

'I don't need the details,' Haley said. 'The past is the past. We don't get it back, however hard we try.'

'I wish . . .' Zoey began, but her sentence wound down like a clockwork toy and no one ever knew what it was she wished.

'Listen to me,' Haley whispered, gently putting her hand under Zoey's chin and raising her head. 'Look ahead. Don't look back.'

I called Mrs Bishop to say I'd bring Zoey home. We drove by Hartmann, most of the time in silence until I parked the car on an overlook which took in the whole of the lake, glistening in the sun.

'I'd like for there to be reasons,' Zoey began. She leaned her head against the warm leather of the headrest, half closing her eyes.

'For what?' I took my shades out of the vanity shelf, put them on, then took up the same position.

'For all of this. Jonas, Arizona . . .'

'Summer and Phoenix,' I added. 'Four in one year. What are the odds?'

Zoey sighed. 'If we only knew why.'

The sun was hot. It bounced off the red hood. 'I know. We all want it to make some kind of sense. But maybe it's just random.'

'That's too scary.' She stared at the lake in the distance. 'How come Arizona could drown in something that beautiful?'

'Questions, questions!' I complained. It was time to sidetrack again. 'That's an eagle up there – see.'

The bird soared on a warm current of air, the tips of its wing feathers spread wide. Then it tilted and dropped from the thermal, hovering over one spot, ready to swoop.

'I don't believe she did it.' Zoey turned her head towards me.

We were treading on thin ice again. I hid my edgy reaction behind my dark glasses.

'She didn't kill herself – no way!'

'They say she did.'

'Who's "they"? People in the town. Journalists. What do they know?'

It had been on TV and in the papers – a second fatality at Ellerton High. This time, a drowning, and it looked like suicide. That's what the forensic report had suggested.

'They didn't know Arizona the way we did.' Zoey watched the eagle drop to the ground. It flew up again with a small animal draped from its hooked beak. 'For a start, if she'd wanted to kill herself, it wouldn't have been in water.'

It was no good – I was trying to resist but I couldn't *not* speculate. 'I hear you. You're saying Arizona was a great swimmer, she snorkelled, she was a scuba diver—'

'No, not that. I mean, Arizona had a big thing about her hair and make-up, remember. Her appearance in general. And she was pretty much into the drama of every occasion. If she knew someone was going to find her dead, she'd make darned sure she was looking good.' Zoey paused then blushed. 'Am I as mean as I made that sound?' she asked.

'Yep,' I grinned. 'But I totally agree.' *And she hasn't changed any*, I wanted to add. *Last time I saw her, among the*

Beautiful Dead out at Foxton Ridge, she was still the same high-maintenance drama queen.

I chewed my lip. *Don't talk about it, don't even go near.* And to remind me, Hunter sent the million winged souls fluttering around my head, making me dizzy, forcing me to sit up straight in my driver's seat.

'So you agree – she didn't plan to do it?' Zoey's theory had brought her upright too.

I shrugged. The wings were still with me. They didn't scare me any more, but I was definitely paying attention. 'What am I – a mind-reader?' I protested.

'Think about it, Darina. Would anybody who was sane head all the way out here, knowing that she had no car to drive because it was in the garage waiting to be fixed, so she had to walk a distance of – what, three whole miles, which everybody knows Arizona had never done in her entire life . . . ?'

'OK.' I put both hands up in surrender. I was practically deafened by Hunter's winged warning not to betray the Beautiful Dead. 'I don't want to talk about it.'

'Darina!' Zoey let me know I was letting her down.

I shook my head and turned the ignition key. 'Like Mrs Jonson said, the past is the past.'

We don't get it back, she'd added. Only I knew we could, or at least the Beautiful Dead could – and did. The wings beat like crazy as I backed off from the overlook and swung on to the road.

Hi, *good to hear from you at last,* I said to the wings. I'd dropped Zoey off at her place and was heading home. *I was worried crazy in case you never came back.*

I drove with the top down and they fluttered around my head in a feathery flurry, more a reminder than a warning now. *Do you know how many times I've driven out to Foxton lately? Yeah, I guess you do.*

I stopped at a red light and glanced sideways. 'Phoenix!'

He was sitting in the seat Zoey had just vacated, waiting for me to see him and giving me his crooked smile.

'Jeez!' I cried. The light turned green and I eased the car across the junction, too slow for the guy behind me, who almost rammed my back fender.

'Phoenix, don't do that! Don't just *appear!*'

'So you want me to go away again?' he asked in that lazy, mumbling voice. 'I can do that!' He got ready to dematerialize.

'No, don't! Listen, you almost gave me a heart attack. Let me turn off the road.' I fumbled with the controls, finally jerking to a stop in a small parking lot outside a general grocery store.

'Hey, Darina.' Phoenix grinned.

I put my hand out to touch him, to check he was, you know, real.

He grabbed my hand. 'Long time, huh?'

'For ever,' I breathed. I'd been counting the days, the hours and minutes. But now Phoenix was here, I was having trouble finding something meaningful to say. Instead I stared down at our two hands, his big and broad, mine smaller and smoother, enjoying the feel of his thumb stroking my palm.

'Hunter made us stay away,' he told me. 'You know how he is.'

'A control freak,' I muttered.

'Yeah, I could make a zombie joke about him being heartless . . .'

'Don't!'

'Bad taste?'

I nodded. No feelings, literally no heart – that's how it was when you came back from the dead. And a skin so pale it looks like sunlight never touched it.

Phoenix's beautiful, smooth face made my own heart beat fast enough for the two of us.

'I'm here now,' he said softly.

Then he made me move out of the driver's seat and he took my place. Without saying anything, he drove on to a road that led out of town so that five minutes later we'd left the houses behind and were heading down the dirt track that led to our favourite spot by Deer Creek.

As the car bumped and jolted, I stared up at the sky. Not a cloud in sight, no breeze. That's if you needed a weather report right now.

Phoenix parked the car by the creek, near to a bunch of thick, low-growing golden willows. Again he grabbed me by the hand, this time to pull me out of the car and lead me past the willows to a rocky ledge overlooking the water. We stood side by side, arms around each other's waists, staring down.

The water was so clear you could see each pebble resting on the bed of the creek. It flowed smoothly, carrying the first leaves of fall on its eddying surface.

Then we sat on the rock to catch the last rays of the sun, Phoenix with his long legs crooked and offering me space to sit in between, resting my back against his chest. His arms encircled me.

'I missed you,' I murmured. Which didn't go any way towards describing the gaping gash in my heart, the nights of black loneliness with no one to lead me out of despair.

I twisted round to see his face – features that didn't quite fit the beauty stereotype, though his high forehead and cheekbones missed it by a millimetre and those big, blue-grey eyes hit it right on target. No, it was the mouth that made him different – just that downward turn at one corner and the way his full lips moved around those laid-back, drawled words.

He leaned forward to kiss me.

Again! Again! my body sighed. It was all I wanted. Nothing else mattered, lips to lips, shared breaths, seeing him up close and blurred through a fringe of dark lashes.

Phoenix pulled me back against a bank of long, dried grass and kissed me harder. I went headlong with the surge of love, stronger and more dangerous than the current of any mountain creek.

Then suddenly Phoenix broke off and pulled his head away from me. His eyes narrowed and he raised his hands to keep me at a distance.

'What happened?' I looked around. Had someone crept up on us? What was the matter? 'Don't tell me – Hunter. Is he here?'

Phoenix shook his head. 'No – yeah. I mean, he's *always* here.'

'The overlord,' I muttered. The red-hot passion was cooling fast, I was back in control. 'Dude, he's better than any other form of birth control!'

We laughed. Then we grew serious again.

'There's a rule,' Phoenix explained. 'I can't . . . you know . . . give myself totally. We need to keep a distance.'

'Says who? Hunter? Doesn't he know that rules are made to be broken?'

Hunter was way worse than Laura and Jim. Or I should say, his sanctions were a whole lot tougher. If I stayed out late, Laura could still ground me – it was her house, she paid the bills, etcetera. But obeying the rules gave Phoenix his only chance to set the record straight – if he overstepped the mark set down by his overlord, he got kicked out of Foxton and was back in limbo, period. And if I listened hard right now, I could hear the wings of a million lost souls in limbo beating and begging to take his place.

'OK.' I nodded. *No contest.*

Phoenix closed his eyes. 'You understand,' he sighed. 'You know how hard this is for me?'

'I do,' I whispered. 'From now on, I promise to keep my hands off you!'

The humour this time was less belly-laugh, more bitter-sweet. 'What did I do to deserve this?' he asked, grabbing my hands and refusing to let me move away. 'I mean you, Darina. You're the most beautiful thing I ever saw, plus I never know what crazy thing you're going to do or say next. You always catch me off guard.'

'And you the mind-reader,' I kidded. I felt myself falling away swiftly into the dark, lonely place and heaved myself back by switching the topic. 'So tell me how come Hunter permitted you to show up at last?'

Phoenix shrugged. 'He never gives reasons. The truth is he only showed up again earlier today. I don't know where he's been hanging out since the Jonas thing.'

'So where were you and the others?' I asked. Not at Foxton, I was certain.

He was uneasy and looked away. 'Arizona took control. She said we had to leave Foxton for a while, let things get back to normal around here.'

'So where did you go?' I insisted.

'A couple of places I'd never been before – I can't tell you exactly.'

I did the tutting thing. 'You mean "won't". As in, it's another of Hunter's rules.'

'All I know is Hunter went off and Arizona took care of us and warned us not to ask any questions.'

'OK, you don't need to answer, but let me take an educated guess. Hunter went back to limbo to update whoever or whatever it is he answers to – like, an overlord-overlord. He left the Beautiful Dead in some secret hiding place, kind of hibernating until he made it back to the far side.' I studied Phoenix's face for a reaction

24

but didn't find one, which meant I was right. 'That's interesting. There's someone or something telling Hunter what to do. And listen, Phoenix, I don't want to hear you telling me not to worry my pretty head over these things – OK?'

'As if.' He leaned back and rested his hands behind his head. 'What a waste of energy that would be.'

'So what was it like, taking orders from Arizona?' There was an edge to this question, I admit.

'Arizona's cool. She's real smart.'

'Should I be jealous?' I only half kidded. After all, I knew a dozen boys at Ellerton High who'd been into Arizona's looks and style, even if her frosty personality had been about as inviting as skinny-dipping in an icy lake. Like Phoenix, all the male students admired her from afar.

'As if,' he repeated. 'But seriously – you don't want to mess with her, OK?'

'No, I only have to save her zombie soul.' I reminded him of the baseline reason we were here. 'A lot of people are turning their attention to Arizona since the mystery surrounding Jonas was cleared up. Zoey, for one.'

Phoenix sat up straight. 'She's asking questions?'

'Yes, and don't worry, I didn't share any secrets. Hunter and a million wings made sure of that.'

He relaxed again.

'Zoey is saying she doesn't believe Arizona drowned herself, and she doesn't think it was an accident either. And I guess she may be right.'

'You do?' Mister Cautious gave nothing away, reminding me there were things he couldn't share, even with me.

'Yeah. Otherwise why would Hunter choose her to return to the far side?' I knew the overlord only dealt with injustice and doubt – the random shooting of Summer Madison by an unknown gunman, Phoenix's death by stabbing in a fight between gangs. A straightforward, explicable death didn't deserve all this special attention. 'She's Beautiful Dead because there's a mystery.'

We sat in silence for a while, watching the endless flow of water at our feet.

'Darina, you really don't have to do this.' When he spoke, Phoenix had moved away into some remote head space. 'There's a good chance we can find out what happened without you.'

I reacted like I'd been stung. 'Yeah – like the Beautiful Dead have had eleven months plus to do that already, and how far did you get? You don't have much time left, remember.'

How could they forget? A soul can exist for twelve

months in the zombie community, not a day more. The end.

'You still don't have to do it.'

I stood up and balanced, arms wide, right at the edge of the rock. 'What are you saying – that I can have my memory zapped by your superpowers and walk away from here as if you never existed? Good – thanks!'

'The alternative – maybe it's too much to ask.' Phoenix offered me an exit from the craziness but I could see in his eyes that he didn't expect me to grab it. He knew me better.

'When did I ever walk away?' I murmured.

He drew me back from the edge and kissed me gently this time, stroking the back of my neck. 'So you'll help Arizona the way you helped Jonas?'

'Like I'll help Summer and you.'

'Then it's time,' he said, taking me by the hand.

2

The barn out at Foxton was filled with sunlight but I was cold in my T-shirt and jeans. I shivered and stayed close to Phoenix.

'Who's that?' I asked him, pointing to a new guy, who looked as lost and confused as I had been the first time I came across the Beautiful Dead.

Phoenix shook his head. 'I've never seen him before.'

The newcomer sat on the ground in a shadowy corner, hugging his knees to his chest. He looked like he was trying to catch his breath, as if he was in a lot of pain.

'Meet Lee Stone.' Arizona made the introductions among the Beautiful Dead. 'Lee, this is Phoenix Rohr.'

The new guy struggled to his feet. Phoenix stood over six feet, but Lee was taller still. He was broad and strong, with fair hair bleached by the sun, looking like he'd stepped right off a beach.

'Summer, come and say hi to Lee,' Arizona invited. She drew my old buddy into the tight circle, excluding me by turning her back.

Phoenix realized it and made room for me. 'Hey, Lee, this is Darina.'

The poor guy could hardly stand. He hadn't any idea where he was and there was no Californian tan to match the muscles and the bleached hair.

'It's OK. Everything's cool,' Summer assured him. Her blonde hair shone like gold in the sunlight. She was wearing a loose, light white cotton smock and jeans.

Lee didn't speak. Fear and pain were written all over his face.

'What's happening?' I whispered to Summer. The cold seemed to intensify, though the sun still shone.

'We're waiting for Hunter.'

I shivered – partly because of the lack of heat, partly at the sound of the overlord's name. I felt Phoenix grasp my hand and keep a firm hold.

'So don't ask any more questions,' Arizona warned. 'Because we don't have the answers.'

As we waited, more familiar figures appeared. There was Eve with baby Kori, drifting in from the yard. Donna came down the rickety stairs from the hayloft. Eve and Donna were Hunter's right-hand helpers – always on guard and ready to set up the force field to repel far-siders. So far I've never asked their histories and they never speak of it. Right now, no one said a word.

So I had a long time to figure things out. Poor Lee might be sinking under a landslide of confusion, but I could coolly put the pieces together. Young guy, tall and athletic, in pain and confused. Who did that remind me of when I first came to the barn, a lifetime ago? Young guy, recently dead, pale and perfect, taking his first faltering steps out of limbo into the far-side world of the Beautiful Dead, like Phoenix before him.

All I had to do now was find the death mark on that smooth, cold skin.

A shadow fell across the entrance to the barn. We all turned as Hunter appeared.

He was straighter, sterner even than I remembered. Not a single muscle moved in his stony features as he walked towards Lee and his deep-set eyes took in every detail. 'You made it back,' he noted.

'What is this? What happened?' Lee had caught his breath and looked ready to flee or to fight, he hadn't decided which.

'Take it easy,' Hunter told him. 'Right now you're hurting, but you're safe here with us.'

His words seemed to calm Lee, who took his first real

look around the circle, taking in Summer and Arizona, Eve and the baby, Donna, Phoenix and me. 'This is too weird,' he muttered. 'Last thing I know I was on the slopes with my snowboard . . .'

'And now you're here,' Hunter said. 'Here is what matters. You have something important to work out and we'll help you do that.'

'I was alone on the slope, the first one up there.' Past trauma – the ultimate and irreversible one – still demanded Lee's attention. 'Blue skies, perfect snow, then all of a sudden—'

'The light went out,' Arizona interrupted. 'And you don't know what went wrong. There's a blank in your memory big enough to swallow you whole and so much pain you can hardly bear it. We know.'

'We need to welcome you,' Hunter told him. He made Lee stand in the centre of the circle and strip off his shirt, then he turned his head towards me. 'Darina, you can leave now. Wait in the house.'

Phoenix smiled at me and nodded, then I felt his grasp slacken. Even though I wanted to argue with Hunter about staying I felt his stern eyes bore through me and the urge dissolved. Minus my willpower, I left the barn without uttering a word.

Hunter didn't say anything about not turning and

looking over my shoulder though. Halfway across the yard, I took a peek.

Lee was in the centre of the ring and the Beautiful Dead were chanting, their voices soft and rhythmic, their expressions welcoming. The delicate features of Summer's face especially seemed to light up, her eyes were shining, her hair floating around her shoulders. Next to her, Arizona had peeled away all those layers of bitter sarcasm and allowed an open contentment to take over her whole body. Eve, with her baby in her arms, closed her eyes in a trance.

Darina, wait in the house! Hunter stood with his back to me, but he had eyes in the back of his head. And he didn't need to speak out loud to dish the orders. Like a robot I turned and walked on.

But I did hear the chanting as I stepped up on to the house porch, and I heard Phoenix's voice among all the rest, saying, 'Welcome, Lee. Welcome to the world of the Beautiful Dead.'

They did their zombie thing, then Summer came to the house to fetch me. 'So, Darina, how are you?' she asked.

I shook my head. 'How long have you got?'

'OK, stupid question.' She tapped the arm of the rocking-chair to set it in motion. Backwards, forwards, like the ticking of an old clock. 'Have you seen my parents lately?'

'No, I haven't been out your side of town.'

'My mother doesn't leave the house much,' Summer confided. 'It's seven and a half months since I left, and she stays inside.'

I told her that her mom still needed recovery time. 'Your dad takes care of her. He saw Laura in the mall and told her he works at home now. He doesn't need to go to the office.'

'Still dreaming up homes for people,' Summer smiled. 'As a little kid I loved to watch him draw those plans, those magical lines and angles. It's his way of making dreams come true.'

'He's a great architect,' I agreed. I knew Mr Madison had designed the house Zoey and her family lived in, plus most of the expensive homes in the Westra neighbourhood, including the Taylor place, which had once featured in an edition of *Mountain Living*.

Weirdly, the Madisons' own home wasn't a big deal. Sure, it was large and it had windows down to the ground on the side of the house that overlooked Amos Peak, and you could see forest and hills for miles. But the interior was cluttered and homey, crammed with Summer's musical instruments and colourful, half-finished paintings stacked against the wall.

'I'm glad Dad's working,' Summer sighed. 'Is Mom still painting? No, you don't know. I forgot.'

Back and forth, back and forth went the chair. A slight frown marked Summer's smooth, pale forehead.

'So Lee joined your group,' I noted. With Summer I never run at stuff like I usually do. She slows me down and makes me feel like I want to take care of her, even now. And we find the time to talk.

'He needs answers.' Summer went to the window and looked out across the yard. 'Dying alone on a ski slope at the age of nineteen – that's tough.'

Like getting caught in a random shooting in a mall isn't! I thought of Summer's manner of departing this life at the hands of an unknown psychopath. 'Did you see Lee's death mark?'

'At the base of his spine, a perfect pair of angel wings,' she told me. 'Don't worry about Lee, Darina. Hunter will look out for him. It's Arizona we have to focus on right now.'

'I know.' I paced the small room from door to stairway. 'This won't be easy,' I admitted. 'Arizona's hard to like.'

'Who says you have to like her?' Summer gave me one of her wide, open smiles. 'All you have to do is find out what really happened and set her free.'

34

'With Jonas it wasn't difficult,' I tried to explain. 'Everyone loved him. I don't understand – why does Arizona act so harsh?'

'Because!' Summer opened the door to let the sun slant across the faded rug. 'Just don't take it personally.'

I laughed. 'It *is* personal! Didn't you see the way she just cut me out of your circle?'

'So try not to react. Chill. Think about it, Darina, Arizona's used to looking like she's in control.'

'But not this time, huh? For once she has to rely on someone.'

'And that someone is you.' Summer nodded. '*Now* do you get it?'

'Darina, are you ready?' Arizona demanded.

I was sitting with her and Phoenix on the steps to the hayloft, maybe thirty minutes after my conversation with Summer. The afternoon light was already fading and every centimetre of me was wishing it was just me and Phoenix on those stairs.

'What is this, the hundred-metre sprint?' Summer had said not to react, but there was an energy between me and Arizona that meant conflict, like putting two chemicals into a Petri dish and standing back to watch the reaction.

Arizona glared at me. 'Hunter said for me to give you

the key facts. Here they are. It was late October, Thursday, not a warm day. I don't remember planning to go for a swim.'

Ha-ha! 'Did you meet anyone? Who did you speak with?' I asked.

'My parents, I guess. I don't recall. Dad was busy that morning so I skipped class and took my car for repair.'

'In town?'

She nodded and failed to meet my gaze. 'Some place behind the mall. I don't remember the name.'

'Did anyone go with you?' I had to squeeze real hard to get the details. 'Who gave you a ride home?'

'I didn't go home.'

Phoenix punctured the silence that followed. 'Give Darina a break,' he told Arizona. 'She's having a hard time here.'

'And I'm not?' she spat back at him, and for a moment they did their silent zombie mind-reading deal. Angry looks shot between them but I wasn't included in the unspoken exchange.

I always think of Arizona as someone you would spot in a style magazine – tight-fitting T-shirt and jeans, boots with heels that make her taller, skinnier still. Her face is framed by long, silky black hair. She has eyes the colour of green glass and a scornful pout to her full lips.

What had I learned about the way she died? I had a car service garage without a name, a time of day. Not a lot. And it had been like extracting teeth. I was glad when we were interrupted.

'Hey, Darina,' Iceman said, as he walked into the barn. 'I just came back from Government Bridge.'

Then I realized Iceman hadn't been part of the welcoming committee for Lee Stone. All the Beautiful Dead had gathered, except for him. How could I have overlooked him, another guardian, along with Eve and Donna?

'Hey, Iceman,' I replied with an embarrassed smile.

'Hunter sent me down there to check out the guys at the new engineering works,' he explained. 'I didn't like what I saw.'

'How many people?' Phoenix asked.

'Five – one surveyor and four guys to do the work. And a whole heap of machinery – diggers and flatbed trucks, mainly. They plan to strengthen the bridge, starting today.'

Government Bridge was a couple of miles downstream from where we sat – a creaky wooden structure that groaned under the weight of SUVs driven by the hunters and picnickers. It was National Forest territory and evidently someone in the planning section had decided it needed an overhaul before winter set in.

'What makes you think they'll head this way?' Arizona wanted to know. Her tone suggested she didn't understand what was the big deal. 'OK, so the creek here runs on down to Government Bridge, but I wouldn't have those guys down as students of the local flora and fauna.'

In other words, the workers dug holes and sank steel supports into the ground, then in the evening they drove straight to the nearest bar.

'Exactly – our creek runs under the bridge,' Iceman said calmly. 'The surveyor is heading upstream to check water flow as we speak.'

Phoenix stood up and vaulted over the wooden stair rail on to the barn floor. 'Does Hunter know?' he asked.

'I already told him. He said to take you and Arizona with me. We have to cut the guy off before he gets here.'

Straight away everything changed. Arizona dropped the snooty attitude, took a band from her pocket and tied back her hair, ready for action. Phoenix was already out through the door when I sprinted after him and asked if I could come too. 'No, you'd better stay here' was on his lips when Hunter exited the house with Lee Stone. 'Take her,' he told Phoenix curtly from the shadowy porch. 'And take Lee along too. Let him see the way we work.'

So Phoenix, Iceman and Arizona led the way down the

bank of the creek, with me and the rookie zombie on their tails. We trod through long grass, over boulders and through willow thickets, raising a family of mule deer from the bushes, sending them leaping up an almost sheer slope.

'Crap!' Lee swore as he plunged ankle deep into the icy water.

'Keep up!' Arizona ordered as he stooped to unlace his boot. By this time Government Bridge was in sight.

'What is this – my worst nightmare?' Lee muttered. He looked as though someone had hit him on the head and he was still reeling in the after-effect.

'Kind of,' I grunted, pulling myself up the granite rockface to a ledge which kept me clear of the stream. 'But wait – there's more!'

'Keep your head down, Darina!' Arizona hissed. 'Do you want to advertise us and get us all zapped back where we came from?'

'Maybe,' I muttered under my breath.

Fifty metres ahead, Phoenix heard me with his super-hearing and frowned. He pointed to the two yellow earth-movers by the old bridge and a small knot of men standing nearby. 'No sign of the surveyor,' he reported.

'That's not good.' Iceman was sure he'd heard the surveyor tell the guys he was heading upstream. 'Maybe we should cut back and take another look.'

'Not right now,' Arizona contradicted. The light was poor but she'd noticed a worker splitting away from the group and heading towards us. My heart lurched when I saw he was carrying a shotgun.

'What happened, Josh? What did you see?' Another guy yelled after him. A third picked up his own gun from a flatbed truck.

'I thought I saw something – coyote maybe,' the overweight one named Josh called over his shoulder. 'Or maybe a deer.'

Arizona took up position behind a tall rock. 'Thanks, Darina,' she muttered. 'That wouldn't be coyote or deer – that would be you he saw.'

'What you going to do – shoot it?' Josh's buddies laughed at the clumsy run he was making up the hill towards us. 'You planning on mule-deer burger for supper?'

Still, in spite of the laughter, there were two men with guns heading our way. Phoenix knew it was time to get serious.

As I came up beside him and Iceman, crouching low behind a rock weathered into a tall, rounded pinnacle, I felt them set up the zombie force field that had terrified me so many times in the recent past. First there was a fierce wind blowing dirt and grit in a cloud across the

40

hillside, then the sound of sighing, then wings beating louder than you would ever believe.

'Crap!' Lee muttered from somewhere behind me. Shock had cut down his vocabulary, it seemed. 'Is that a giant flock of birds, or what?'

Invisible wings beating up a storm, battering at the guys with guns, forcing them to stoop forwards and stop in their tracks. It grew darker. The guys raised their arms to shield their heads.

'They'll turn around – you watch!' I hissed at Lee.

But not straight away. These were two tough guys.

'Whoo, shi-it!' Josh yelled as the wings raised by Phoenix and Iceman blasted against them. 'This is what those storm chasers go after – can you believe the adrenalin rush?'

'What are we – in the eye of a tornado?' the other man cried. 'Man, that still sounds like wings to me!'

More and more lost souls joined the force field to drive the guys back down to the bridge. They swept across the mountainside, flattening the grass and tearing at flowers, whirling against the outsiders until their legs buckled and they sank to the ground.

'Wait for it – here come the death-heads!' I warned Lee.

These were grown men down there who didn't want to lose face in front of their buddies, but it had grown dark and they were getting battered by a force they didn't understand, being driven back down the hill. And now they were seeing things – nightmarish, unhealthy stuff you didn't admit to after it had happened because people would shun you and call you crazy.

Iceman, Phoenix and Arizona had called in reinforcements. Death-heads appeared in the sky, blurred at first, then taking shape and hovering over the men, swooping down one by one, filling the guys' vision with the yellow domes of skulls and eye sockets so deep, so dark they knocked all sense out of you. I knew – I'd been there.

I watched the men curl up on the ground. The three guys down by the bridge started to run up the hill, then they too felt the wings beat hard and relentless, saw their brave buddies curled up like foetuses, maybe saw, or thought they saw, skulls appearing out of the darkness, and then they didn't come any further. Instead, they turned and ran blindly to their trucks. They didn't wait for the two on the hillside – they started their engines and drove out of there, along the dirt road towards Turkey Shoot Ridge.

Beside me, Lee slowly got a grip on what was happening. 'We can do that?' he muttered. 'We can fetch souls out of hell?'

'Not hell – limbo.' Arizona had to be word perfect, even now. 'Now watch these two – they've had enough.'

She was right. Josh and his buddy had grabbed hold of one another. They raised themselves to their knees with expressions so agonized they didn't look human. They left their guns behind as they slid and stumbled back down the hill.

'Looks like those two get to walk home.' Hunter's calm voice stole up on us from behind. He had a stranger with him – a vacant-looking grey-haired guy with glasses, dressed in a plaid shirt, jeans and hiking boots. 'You too,' he said to his companion.

The man's eyes were glazed. He didn't see or hear anything going on around him.

'Meet the surveyor,' Hunter explained. 'He must have got past you without you knowing. Summer spotted him hiking down the hill towards the barn. There was no other way – I had to wipe the whole episode from his mind.'

If I wanted to be with Phoenix, saving Arizona came as part of the deal. Every time I reminded myself of this, it was like swallowing bitter medicine.

'You take care,' Phoenix told me by the old water tower on Foxton Ridge as we got ready to say goodbye. 'And promise me – don't rush into a situation unless you can see a way out.'

'Since when did I do that?'

'Since the first time we met. It's what makes you interesting.' He was looking deep into my eyes, reading the hurt in my heart. 'Most kids at Ellerton High live life with the brakes on. You don't.'

'And now you're telling me to be like the others,' I sighed. 'Always check things out before I act, look over my shoulder, don't rush. And anyhow it's worse than ever in town now – since, you know . . .'

'The four deaths,' he interpreted. 'A motorcycle crash, a drowning, a shooting and a stabbing. How bad can it get?'

I nodded. 'They think it's going to be them next, and so do their paranoid parents.' Stress levels had hit an all-time high in Ellerton. Kids were getting grounded for the least little thing, parents made curfews that a five-year-old would find hard to keep. 'Every time I grab my car keys, Laura jumps on my back, asking where am I going, who with and what for.'

'So take care,' Phoenix repeated. He was holding my hand loosely now, staring down the slope towards the barn.

I needed his full attention back on me so I put my arms

around his neck. 'What are you thinking?'

'Nothing. It's not important.' His arms came around my waist, but he still wasn't fully there.

I thought a kiss would do it – one of those sad, tender ones for parting when it was the last thing we wanted to do. Wrong again!

'I'm sorry, Darina.' Letting go of me and stepping back, Phoenix refused to meet my gaze. 'Hunter needs me. I have to go.'

I sensed small stabs of panic attack my stomach and chest. Was he withdrawing from the total love I felt for him? If so, what had I said? What had I done? 'I love you,' I whispered.

He looked straight at me now with the faintest shake of his head. Almost no movement at all, but the negative was clear in his eyes. 'I have to leave,' he said again. 'You drive safely, OK?'

I cried myself out before I reached home. I told myself I was being hypersensitive, that Arizona had got under my skin and the arrival of Lee Stone had thrown another unknowable ingredient into the mix.

Driving through Centennial, I got myself back under control. *Next time, Phoenix and I will be cool*, I thought. *I was imagining a problem that wasn't really there. He still loves me as much as I love him, which is totally and for ever.*

'Kim Reiss called,' Laura told me when I threw my keys down on the lobby table and went into the kitchen. 'She brought your appointment time forward to four-thirty Monday afternoon.'

'Do I have to go?' I whined. 'You have to know you're throwing away your hard-earned cash.'

Laura had paid for six sessions of therapy up front and no way would she let me wriggle out of Monday. 'I believe it's helping you come through the trauma,' she insisted.

'Really? How can you tell?'

Laura gave me coffee. 'You don't lie on your bed all day like you did right after the event.'

As in, right after Phoenix died. Thump went my heart and I almost veered back out of control. I'd just left my Beautiful Dead boyfriend on Foxton Ridge with a distance between us and anxiety gnawing at my heart.

Maybe Laura caught the look of pain in my eyes and her voice turned gentle. 'You've started to go out more, Darina. And you give me a hard time, like you always used to – like you're doing right now!'

'OK, I'll see Kim,' I agreed, because it mattered to Laura and because it took attention away from what I was really doing.

* * *

On Sunday I got up early and went round to Logan's place.

'You look like you didn't sleep,' Logan told me before I set foot through the kitchen door. His dad was still in bed. Logan was cooking himself eggs and bacon.

'Thanks,' I told him, taking a glance in the hallway mirror. There were dark circles under my eyes, not helped by the smoky eyeliner and mascara I never left home without.

'Do you want something to eat?'

'No. Thanks.' I sat at the table, accepted a glass of milk, then plunged right in. 'Tell me about your after-school guitar classes with Frank Taylor.'

Blue bacon smoke rose from the pan. Logan liked it crispy. 'You want to improve your guitar?' he asked. 'I can teach you.'

'Sure I want to improve,' I lied. 'But I want to learn from a good teacher, Logan. I hear Mr Taylor is in that category.'

I'd lain awake all night, thinking of ways to get more facts on Arizona so I could move forward. Usually there would be friends I could go to and they would lead me to a whole network of information about who she hung out with, where she went on a regular basis, any secrets she might have kept. But Arizona had been so *not* the type to

47

make close friendships, so that avenue was closed. Which left me with getting closer to her parents and the possibility of finding out more through them. So you see why I was quizzing Logan over his guitar lessons.

I was totally using my old friend, I admit. And no way could I tell him the real reason for my interest.

'Frank Taylor teaches Spanish guitar,' Logan explained. 'You sure you don't want some bacon?'

'Sure. Classical Spanish guitar is what I'm interested in. I already play electric – Jonas taught me, remember?'

'So why don't you let me teach you Spanish?' Logan wouldn't let this drop. 'That way we get to spend time together.'

That's why not, I thought. Logan was like one of those barnacle sea creatures that clamp themselves to the side of a boat. Sailors have to scrape them off. A year ago I wouldn't have said this about him. Twelve months back, Phoenix hadn't come into my life.

'Does Frank Taylor do his private coaching from the music college where he teaches?'

'No, I go round to his house.' Logan made short work of his breakfast. 'Every Tuesday at 6.00 p.m. You should see it, Darina. I mean, compared with this place, even with your place, it's a palace. They took pictures of it for *Mountain Living* after Mrs Taylor brought in a decorator for a whole year. She had the entire place redesigned.'

'I know it. So you go round to his house,' I repeated. *Good*. My mind was made up. 'Thanks, Logan,' I said, standing up and sneaking his last piece of bacon off his plate as I left. 'I'll call there after lunch.'

Frank Taylor definitely didn't need the money, so it must have been pure love of the guitar that made him sell his musical knowledge for a downmarket twenty-five dollars an hour.

I drove to Westra and pulled up outside the electronic gates of 2850 North 22 Street. The Taylor house stood in a big expanse of lawn. It was built Dutch style with curved gables and low roofs, and a fancy carved porch on two sides. A gardener tended the flowerbeds, so I called to him. 'Is Frank Taylor in?'

The old, skinny guy came to the gate and shot me a suspicious look. 'Who's asking?'

'I want to take guitar classes,' I said, without answering directly. Who was this guy, anyway?

'That's OK, Peter.' A tall figure walked down the drive towards us. I would put him at sixty years of age at least, and was surprised when he opened the gate and offered to shake my hand. 'I'm Frank Taylor,' he told me.

Wow, so Arizona's father was a senior citizen! His

shoulders stooped, his grey eyes were set deep in their sockets and surrounded by wrinkles.

'How did you know I give guitar classes?'

'A friend of mine – Logan Lavelle – told me.'

'Yes, Logan's a good kid. He plays with solid technique but without much flair,' Frank let me know. 'So come into the house – er . . . ?'

'Darina.' I followed him up the driveway. 'I knew Arizona. We were classmates.' *Better get that out in the open*, I thought.

'She never spoke of you,' he informed me stiffly. He held the door open for me. 'Come in.'

I stood in a lobby bigger than my entire house. The style was a mix of traditional and contemporary – polished wood and brushed steel surfaces combined, leather sofas big enough to seat a whole basketball team set against neutral beige walls.

'Allyson, this is Darina,' Frank told the woman who stepped out of an inner room. 'She's the same age as Arizona would have been.'

A shiver ran through me – for a second I thought I was looking at Arizona's older sister that I knew nothing about. But then I took in the too-perfect, sleek blonde hair, the careful make-up and the frozen forehead with no frown lines and decided, no – Allyson Taylor must be

Arizona's mom. If I had Frank down as sixty, his wife could be no more than thirty-five.

'Hello, Darina.' Allyson couldn't have been less interested. She walked past me and her husband, right out of the front door. 'Frank, I'm at the studio if you need me.'

'Where else?' He gave an exasperated shrug. 'My wife works at a twenty-four-hour news channel,' he explained. 'Come rain or shine, tornado or hurricane, that's where you'll find her.'

I felt this was too much information, so I focused on the designer furniture as he led me into a room that was obviously his music space. Half a dozen guitars stood to attention against one wall, there were keyboards and computers, monitors and sound systems of every description.

'Are you a total novice, Darina, or do you have some musical knowledge?' Frank asked, sitting behind a desk like an attorney in a court of law.

'I play a little.'

He handed me the nearest acoustic guitar. 'Show me.'

I knew a James Taylor song that my dad taught me when I was ten years old, so I made a random choice, told Frank where I learned it, then fumbled through.

'Like you said – you play a little. Do you know anything else?'

'Some of the tracks from the Johnny Cash album at Fulsom Prison.' How had I got myself into this? I was so embarrassed.

'No Bach or Debussy? Your dad didn't teach you to play like Segovia?'

Was Arizona's father making fun of me? I checked his expression and saw no sign of a sense of humour.

Frank Taylor leaned back in his chair. 'So, Darina, why did you really come to the house?'

It seemed the Taylors were used to people snooping. After the *Mountain Living* feature they'd had a crowd of two-bit journalists beating a path to their door to take more pictures for their magazines. Then after the Arizona tragedy, her so-called friends crawled out of the woodwork – rubber-neckers wanting to be close to the action. Or so Mr Taylor told me, and he'd straight away put me into this category. 'If you hadn't mentioned Logan, I wouldn't even have let you through the door,' he added.

'It's not what you think.' We were out in the hallway, I was tripping over a designer settee. 'I do – I *did* know Arizona. We were friends.'

Frank Taylor was out of patience. 'Like I said – she never talked about you. You never came here before today. Arizona's been dead almost a year and there's nothing more for you to find out, so I'm asking you to leave.'

'I'm sorry. I didn't mean to upset you.'

'You haven't,' he told me calmly as he opened the door and showed me out.

The door clicked and I faced the long walk down the drive.

That went really well, I told myself, looking out for Peter the gardener and expecting another dose of humiliation. Peter wasn't around, but there was someone sitting in a summer house in the middle of the lawn – a boy stooped over a large pad of paper that rested on his knee, so busy with his pencil that he didn't notice me.

I heard a door round the side of the main house open and Peter the gardener's voice. 'Raven, where are you?'

The boy raised his head and, in what looked like an overreaction to the hired help's question, stepped out of the summer house to make a run for it. He was maybe nine years old, with Arizona's dark colouring and skinny build, but without any of the Taylor confidence – totally the opposite, in fact. He seemed scared, disorientated, not sure which way to run. And he dropped his pad and paper on the lawn so I hurried across to pick it up for him. 'Here,' I said, offering it back.

I caught a glimpse of the line drawing he'd been making – a detailed, realistic representation of the big house, everything perfectly to scale, drawn freely as if the pencil had never left the paper.

'Raven, I warned you not to leave the house.' Peter appeared round the side of the building. He saw me with the boy and walked sternly towards us.

'Take your drawing,' I urged, pressing it into Raven's hands. 'It's beautiful.'

My words didn't get through the scared-rabbit-caught-in-a-headlight look. He crumpled the drawing and stuffed it into my jacket pocket.

'Come with me, Raven,' Peter said firmly. 'Your dad was asking where you were.'

3

'It was so totally weird,' I told Kim Reiss the next day. 'I didn't even realize that Arizona had a brother.'

'Did you know her well?' My therapist seemed more interested in my relationship with Arizona than the mysterious Raven.

'*Nobody* knew Arizona. She liked it that way. But even she would let people know she had a brother, you'd think.'

'Why does it bother you so much?'

'The kid was scared. It felt like they were trying to keep him hidden away, and that's not right.'

Kim didn't take her gaze off my face, like she was reading a road map, tracing the direction of my emotions and thoughts. 'Maybe they have their reasons.'

'And then there's this.' I pulled the crumpled drawing from my pocket. 'It's the Taylors' house, accurate

55

down to every last pane of glass.'

The piece of paper drew Kim's attention. She nodded, then handed it back. 'I wonder if Raven lives at home the whole time, or if he's away at school.'

'Even so – why the big secret?' It had bothered me all night and right through my school day. 'And how come the house has been cleared of Arizona memorabilia? I didn't see any photographs of her, and there were none of her things lying around. It was like she never existed.'

'Maybe it hurts too much to have reminders on view. We can't judge the Taylors for that.' Kim glanced at her watch. 'Darina, we've spent a quarter of our time on Arizona's situation and I was wondering if there were other topics you'd like to cover.'

'Where do I begin?' I said with a grimace.

'How are things between you and Laura?'

'The same. She stresses, I back away. End of story.'

'And your friend Logan?'

'Ditto.'

'And how are you handling your emotions over the loss of Phoenix?'

'I get through the day,' I muttered. In the early sessions with Kim I'd spilled my guts – how I still saw Phoenix everywhere: in school, in town, every place I looked. She told me it was a normal part of grieving. But she didn't get it – I meant I literally saw my Beautiful Dead boyfriend, materializing out of nowhere, doing his zombie thing.

That was before I learned I had to keep their secret and carry the weight of it around with me every living moment.

So these days, whenever the topic came up, along came the rush of beating wings – Hunter's warning to stay silent. It was happening now – the flurry of wings about to suffocate me if I opened up to my therapist.

'You know something,' I said, standing up with a sudden jerk and making my chair rock on to its back legs. 'I'm through here.'

Kim's eyes registered mild surprise. 'You want to leave? Our session isn't finished yet.'

'It is,' I argued. 'I only come because Laura set it up. I don't want to do it any more.'

The surprise smoothed out and was replaced by a calm, professional expression. 'I hear you, Darina. I'm sorry you feel this way.'

'It doesn't help,' I cried. 'Talking about Phoenix is too painful – you wouldn't understand.'

Kim stood up too. 'Leave if you need to,' she said quietly. 'But my door's always open.'

'Thanks,' I told her as the wings died down. I was out of there, period. And I wouldn't be back.

Which was a pity, because I really liked Kim Reiss. She and I talked the same language and she didn't put any pressure on me. I could have got used to sharing with her.

I spent the rest of Kim's hour drinking Coke in a small diner out in the Centennial area of town, trying to convince myself not to go back out to Foxton until I'd discovered something useful for Arizona. *Go home*, I told myself. *Get some sleep. Try again tomorrow.*

But I felt the pull of the place, especially when I pictured Phoenix walking that ridge, standing guard against snooping construction workers or any unwary hunting party heading their way. I had an issue with him and we needed to talk it through.

Go home, Darina! I insisted. *What good will it do to drive out there in the dark?*

It was the roar of motorcycle engines that drew me back into the present as a flotilla of Harleys sailed into the parking lot. I recognized Brandon Rohr at the head of the group, and a couple of the other riders as guys who'd been at Bob Jonson's wake.

They dismounted from their bikes and strode into the diner, boots clunking, leather jackets creaking. For a while I thought Brandon wasn't going to say hi but then he came and sat down at my table.

One of the gang went up to the counter to order food. Like Brandon, he was in his early twenties – with Brandon's machismo and then some.

'Hey, Darina.' Brandon took his time to unzip his studded jacket and sling it over the back of his chair. 'How do you like your car?'

'Cool.' It was a pity I hadn't finished my Coke and moved off five minutes earlier. Now I was tied into a conversation I didn't want to have with Phoenix's older brother.

'Hey, Kyle, meet Phoenix's girl. Darina, this is Kyle Keppler.' Brandon introduced his buddy at the counter. 'What do you know – talking with her is like getting blood from a stone.'

'Hey,' Kyle grunted without even turning to face me.

Brandon was on a roll. 'I find Darina the best convertible around and all the girl gives me is one lousy word – "cool".' He leaned across the aisle to draw in a couple of the other guys. 'Byram, Aron – meet Darina.'

I recognized Byram as the older rider who'd been kind to Zoey at Bob Jonson's wake. 'Stick with Brandon – he'll take good care of you,' he'd advised me.

I was practically drowning in male hormone, I can tell you. And, as usual, the connection between Phoenix and his older brother overwhelmed me. It was the same gene pool that had given them their height and broad shoulders, their dark hair and crooked smile.

I have a love-hate thing going with Brandon Rohr. I love him for the fact that he's Phoenix's brother, hate him because he led the fight where Phoenix was killed. I would bet good money that it had been Brandon's reputation that set up bad feeling between the gangs in the first place. Not that I have any proof – only a mass of conflicting information and my own suspicious mind. So, even though Brandon is finding me cars and taking care of me because Phoenix asked him to with his dying breath, it's more hate than love if I'm honest.

'You wouldn't know it, Darina,' Brandon said, putting his arm along the back of Kyle's chair as Kyle sat down next to him, 'but you and my buddy here have something in common.'

I doubted that, and the look on my face told them so.

'Hear me out,' Brandon insisted, keeping me firmly on the hook. 'The thing you share is – you both lost someone close to you.'

I looked down at the table, trying to block out his voice.

'You lost Phoenix, Kyle lost Arizona.'

I looked up with a start. 'You mean . . . no way!' Kyle was a million miles from Arizona's refined type – he was broad-featured, blond-haired and, like I said, twenty-plus. His fingernails were chewed.

'You bet,' Brandon said. 'It's a year and Kyle's still secretly broken up over her. They were together longer than you and my brother, for Christ's sake.'

So now there was a boyfriend *and* a brother I didn't know about – thanks, Arizona!

It was getting late but I left the diner and drove out to Foxton anyway. The first stars appeared in the sky, along with a new moon over the neon cross on Turkey Shoot Ridge. By the time I reached the end of the track and set off on foot towards the water tower hidden among the aspens, I couldn't even see where I was putting my feet.

'Shoot!' I tripped against a rock and scraped my shin. *Next time, wear jeans*, I reminded myself. A short skirt didn't cut it in these conditions, neither did pointy shoes. *And bring a flashlight*, I added.

After a lot of stumbling, I reached the tower, glad of one thing – that there was no force field set up by the Beautiful Dead to keep me out. Tonight I didn't have the energy to battle the wings and the death-heads.

Instead, Hunter had sent the new kid, Lee Stone, to greet me. He stepped out from under the tower without speaking.

I jumped back in shock. 'It's good that I've developed nerves of steel,' I told him. 'Couldn't you give me some warning instead of springing out like that?'

'Hunter said to watch out for you,' Lee said. 'He knew you'd come.'

'Hunter knows everything,' I said drily. 'It's the one thing you can be sure of.'

Up there on the ridge, the stars and moon gave me just enough light to take a closer look at Lee, who was dressed in a dark T-shirt and a jacket I recognized as belonging to Phoenix – most likely the one he was wearing when he was stabbed between the shoulder blades. 'Turn around,' I whispered. Sure enough, there was a jagged tear in the leather. I tried to cover up a small gasp and the shudder that ran through me. 'Where are the others?' I asked.

'They're in the barn, holding some kind of meeting.' Lee looked like he still hadn't got used to the idea of coming back from the dead. 'They said for me to keep a lookout.'

'Well, here I am. Shall we walk down and join them?'

Lee shook his head. 'The meeting isn't for far-siders. It's some kind of ritual they need to go through.'

'What kind of ritual?' It was the first I'd heard of this. And I started to resent Lee blocking my path down the hill. 'I need to talk with Phoenix,' I explained. 'It's personal.'

Lee refused to step aside. 'Hunter said no.'

'Oh well, if the overlord forbids it!' I turned on the sarcasm, even though he didn't deserve it. 'Tell me, Lee. Don't you object to the absence of free will around here?'

'I'm sorry. That's the way it is.' He looked dejected and there was still that edge of confusion in his voice. 'Hunter gives the orders.'

'It's OK, I know.' Closing my eyes for a second, I relented. 'Sorry. Sometimes it's hard to bear.'

'What is?'

'Obeying, keeping secrets, being left out of the loop. Did Hunter say when he would let me speak with Phoenix? If not tonight, then when?'

Lee shook his head. 'I have no idea. Sorry.'

'Don't be. It's not your fault.' For a moment I managed to put myself in Lee's shoes. 'Did they find time to explain things to you?' I asked.

'Some,' he mumbled. 'I found out that I wait in line after Arizona, Summer and Phoenix. Waiting's a tough ask, especially since I know there's something here on the far side that needs an explanation.'

I nodded. 'They have a word – *revenant*. You're back here on a temporary basis, with all these crazy powers.'

Lee's puzzled grin of acknowledgement lifted his face and made me realize for the first time that he was a good-looking guy. 'I could zap your mind and wipe your memory clean, isn't that cool?'

'Yeah, but don't try it,' I said, quickly moving on. 'You have no heartbeat but you do have super-hearing, if that's any consolation.'

'I heard your car way beyond Turkey Shoot,' he confirmed.

'So you're one of the Beautiful Dead.' I looked directly into his eyes and the conversation slowed as I reached forward to put a sympathetic hand on Lee's arm. 'Don't worry. It'll make sense in the end.'

'Aah, sweet!' Arizona said, stepping out of the shadows. 'I'm sorry – did I interrupt something?'

I withdrew my hand as if Lee's arm was red-hot.

'So how come you never told me you had a baby brother?' I challenged. 'The same goes for the boyfriend with the muscles, Kyle Keppler!'

Arizona hadn't given me any answers, naturally. She'd body-swerved my big questions and told me that their ceremony was over and Hunter had given permission for me to go down and meet with Phoenix.

'Boy, Darina, do *you* have some explaining to do!' she'd

64

laughed, turning the tables on me as she led me and Lee through the barn door.

The barn was lit with oil lamps that cast flickering shadows over the walls and floor. Most of the Beautiful Dead were still there, though Hunter was missing, I noticed.

Phoenix sat quietly on the hayloft steps, with Eve and baby Kori. Seeing me, he stood up and came across, took my hand and walked me out into the dark night.

'We need to talk,' we both said in the same instant, then we smiled awkwardly.

He took me towards the house, where he picked up another oil lamp before we walked on along the creek.

'What's happening?' I asked, hardly recognizing my own quiet, shaking voice. I felt small under the vast sky. Phoenix's hand was cold as the icy stream. 'I told you I loved you and you didn't tell me back. Why was that?'

He refused to look at me. 'You explain it to me, Darina.'

Speak your fear. Get it out in the open. 'I need to know – am I losing you? Did you stop loving me?' If he said yes, my world would end. Everything would come crashing down. But still I had to know.

Phoenix let go of my hand and walked a little way ahead. 'What makes you say that?'

'You're blocking me, you're not sharing. I never felt you keeping me at this distance before.' Hearing him take a deep breath, I caught up with him. 'I've thought of everything these last two days – maybe there was something I did wrong, I don't know. Or maybe it's you, Phoenix. Is this what happens to the Beautiful Dead? When you first come back to the far side you have feelings the way you used to. You still loved me. But gradually, bit by bit, those human feelings fade and you can't do anything to stop it. Is that what's happening between us? If it's true, I can't bear it, but you have to tell me so that I understand.'

The light flickered over his lovely, smooth face, his eyes shadowed, a small nerve in his forehead jumping. 'You think I don't love you?' he murmured, as if the words were spoken in a foreign language he didn't understand. The creek ran at our feet, shining silver under the stars.

My heartbeat quickened. There'd been some mistake. Everything was going to be cool.

'This isn't easy,' Phoenix confessed. 'The last time you came, I thought you were the one who seemed different. I couldn't get through.'

'You didn't try,' I recalled. 'It was you. You weren't letting me in.'

'Lee arrived. Stuff was happening.'

'You wouldn't look at me. I was scared.'

66

'You seemed distant. I read what you were thinking and I saw your mind was all on him.'

I sprang to my own defence. 'Lee was in pain. You remember that first journey back from limbo – you said it hurt like hell.'

'He noticed you from the start. He liked you, Darina. I saw inside his head too.'

'You're blaming *me* for that!'

'Arizona noticed it too.'

'You talked to her about me? You let her misread the situation and get to you!' Everything wasn't going to be cool after all. We were splitting apart, flailing our arms like drowning men.

Phoenix dropped the oil lamp and began to run up the hill.

I watched him go. What was he talking about – me, Lee, Arizona, liking and loving? 'This is crazy. I thought you people were Grade A mind-readers!' I yelled after him. 'Not drop-out failures!'

Phoenix had broken free and was picking up speed. I began to follow. 'You imagine I have feelings for Lee?' I cried. 'How shallow does that make me?'

He stopped running until I came within ten paces. 'What am I saying? What am I doing?' he begged through breathless gasps.

'You're crazy.' And my faith was shaking, my trust was being stretched.

'Darina, I thought – I was afraid . . .'

'Of losing me?' I realized in a flash. 'No way, Phoenix.'

He came slowly towards me. 'Every time you go away, I feel I can't bear it. It rips me apart.'

'Me too.'

Closer and closer under a million stars. 'It's too difficult. Sometimes I think I'll leave the far side – just give in and go back.'

'Don't!' I pleaded. I caught hold of the collar of his jacket.

'I think of you back in Ellerton, living your life. All I want is to be with you.'

'Don't!' My voice broke down completely.

'I don't want anyone – any other guy – to come near you.'

'I won't let them,' I promised.

He held me too tight. 'I love you and I can't have you.'

I eased free and took his hand, placing it over my heart. 'Don't speak any more,' I pleaded.

It was only then that we noticed small yellow flames on the hillside where Phoenix had dropped the lamp. They licked at the dry grass and thorn bushes, darting across the ground in quick, flickering fingers.

Then Hunter came running out of the darkness below, taking off his jacket and using it to beat down the fire until it died in a shower of red sparks and a cloud of smoke.

Hunter stood astride the burnt patch of ground, arms folded. There was so much anger in his face that I had to take a step back to protect myself.

'Did you ever see a forest fire take hold?' he asked us. 'Do you know how fast it travels?'

'We're sorry,' I stammered. '*I'm* sorry. It was my fault.'

Phoenix came and stood between me and Hunter. 'Don't listen to her. It was me – I dropped the lamp.'

'You think I care about the details?' Hunter's voice stayed threateningly calm as he walked slowly towards Phoenix. Still I expected his rage to explode. 'There are more important things here. Did I say that you could bring Darina out here?'

Phoenix shook his head. 'You said to talk with her in the house, but we needed space so I decided to walk by the stream.'

'*You* decided?' Hunter turned the phrase around on his tongue. 'Since when did you get that kind of choice?'

I was shaking now – he was still stony calm but the anger burned like those flames, deep inside him.

Phoenix didn't answer. Power seemed to be seeping from his body.

'Man, I ought to finish this,' Hunter sighed, walking towards Phoenix. 'What's to stop me zapping you out of here, right back where you belong?'

'No, don't!' I cried, rushing forward to seize Hunter's arm, only to find myself swept back as if I weighed no more than a feather. I fell into the warm ashes on the ground. Phoenix made as if to run towards me, but his legs buckled and he fell to the knees.

'I gave the order,' Hunter reminded Phoenix, summoning up a storm of invisible wings to reinforce what he was saying. 'Word for word, I told you, "Take Darina to the house. Talk with her, find out what her problem is." Simple enough, even for you.'

Phoenix got back on his feet, his head raised and chin jutting out, like a condemned man determined to look death in the face. 'It turned out it wasn't her problem, it was mine. I wasn't thinking clearly.'

'I told you – spare me the details.' Hunter had never looked so unforgiving. 'You overrode the order, came up here, lost control of the situation and started a fire that could have brought the whole county fire service down on us. So tell me, Phoenix, what is it about this story that should make me want to keep you on the far side?'

'Don't send him away,' I pleaded. 'If you do, I won't help any of you!'

There was no reaction, except Hunter turned to me with a look of mild curiosity. 'You have too high an opinion of your own value, Darina.'

'You need me,' I insisted. 'I'm your link to the far side – the only one you can trust.'

'Tell that to Arizona,' he muttered. 'I gather she's still waiting for your so-called help.'

'That's not fair. Arizona hides things from me.' I changed tactics and now I had Hunter's full attention. He became extra alert and his eyes stared into mine. 'It's almost like she doesn't want me to succeed.'

Hunter frowned, then told Phoenix to walk down the hill ahead of us. 'Arizona's future is on the line,' he reminded me. 'Her *eternal* future. So what is she holding back on and why?'

The 'what' I could explain on that dark walk under the stars – namely Raven Taylor and Kyle Keppler, but not her reasons. 'I don't understand the way her mind works,' I told him.

He stopped short of the old truck parked for ever beside the decaying house. 'You're too simple,' he sighed. 'And Arizona's way too subtle. That's part of the problem we're dealing with here.'

'So why the big secrets?' Arizona and I were sitting in the cab of the old truck, staring up at the stars when I challenged her head on.

Hunter had left us there with strict instructions to engage in some plain talking. I felt pretty sure he was now with Phoenix, handing out the punishment for the fire incident. What if he did zap him back into limbo and I never saw Phoenix again? Hunter was definitely powerful enough to do it. *Focus!* I told myself. *Listen to Arizona's excuses.*

'Which secrets are we talking about here?' As always, she was in control, pushing the question back at me, testing me out.

'Let's start with Raven. Tell me about him.'

'What's to tell? He's nine years old. He likes to sketch in a notebook. Period.'

'Why is he so scared?' I cut through the crap and the winding mind game she was playing.

Arizona drummed the hollow dashboard with the fingers of her right hand. 'He thinks the world is a dangerous place for people like him.'

'What do you mean – people like him?'

'People who don't come out of the womb the same as everyone else, whose brains are wired differently – that's

72

supposing that there is such a thing as a normal brain, which I doubt.'

'Stop. Don't go weird and theoretical on me. We're talking about your brother here. I saw him in your garden. What's he afraid of?'

Arizona turned her head towards me. 'Everything,' she said quietly.

I waited for more.

'Watch me,' she said.

I watched.

Arizona narrowed her eyes and frowned deeply. 'What kind of mood am I in right now?'

'Cut it out. Answer my question.'

'I am.' She switched off the frown and replaced it with a smile. 'Now, am I happy or sad?'

'Answer the question!'

'The point is, *you* know – you can read my face, right? Well, my brother can't do that. He can't tell you what a smile means, or when you're about to get mad with him, or if you plan to be kind. His brain can't work it out. So he plays safe and decides to suspect everyone all of the time.'

'That's crazy,' I breathed. The superior, arched-eyebrow look Arizona dealt me made me regret my choice of words. 'I mean, what's that about? Is it an illness?'

'Only if you don't understand it.' Her tone changed and she was softer. 'I never think of my little brother as sick. He's just the way he is – mad at the world, and who can blame him?'

'But your parents – they've decided he needs treatment?'

'Yeah. Ever since Raven was little they've taken him to specialist brain doctors in practically every state. He's been through all the therapies – conventional, alternative, experimental, cutting edge, plain crazy – you name it.'

'And?'

She shrugged. 'They each stick another label on him and send him back home. Or they keep him in a hospital, or lately they send him to autism school. And all Raven wants is to be able to draw his sketches and be left alone.'

'Wow.' The picture she'd painted was pretty painful. What must 'home' be like with a problem like that going on? 'How about your parents? What do *they* want?'

Arizona's fingers tapped more slowly against the dash. 'For it not to have happened,' she murmured. Then *tap-tap* – upped the tempo. 'Which is why they send him away to school.'

'Raven – is he . . . lonely?' I tried to get my head around the situation, remembering the dark-haired, dark-eyed, good-looking, terrified kid in the Taylors' summer house.

Her sigh went on for a long time. 'Sure,' she admitted. 'Now that I'm gone, Raven has no one in the world to root for him.

'So now you know.' Arizona's defences were back up and we were out of the truck and walking on to the porch, looking up at the dark sky. There was still no sign of Hunter or of Phoenix. 'That's why I came back to the far side. I need Raven to know I would never – *never* do what they said I did at Hartmann Lake.'

'You mean, you wouldn't deliberately leave him.' I understood this much at least.

She nodded. 'Especially not now.'

I waited on the porch for her to explain. 'Why not now?' I had to prompt.

'Now that Dad's finally filing for divorce.'

The new information slammed into my brain. 'So when they split, who will get Raven? – Is that what you mean?'

Another nod and the longest of sighs. 'Who will even care?' she added, disappearing into the house and closing the door behind her.

Hunter found me alone on the porch.

'I had no idea what kind of problems she was dealing with,' I told him.

'What – Arizona doesn't come across as a victim?' he asked, smiling without any humour in his eyes. 'But with her family history I guess she is.'

'Her parents seemed so together. Her dad teaches music in college, her mom works as a broadcaster in TV.'

'Did you ever meet them?'

'Not before yesterday. And I only saw Allyson Taylor for a couple of seconds – she was on her way to work. Her dad is way older than I thought. They don't go together as a couple.'

'So your job is to help her brother come through this,' Hunter reminded me. 'You have to get some truth into the situation and find a way of communicating it to the boy.'

'Then will Arizona be able to rest?'

'Maybe. Anyway, her job here will be done. Raven will know that she loved him and didn't want to leave.'

I could see how this might work, but in my opinion it wasn't a whole lot of comfort. The boy would still be wired up wrong. He would still be totally alone.

'Don't question it, Darina,' Hunter read my mind. 'Just do it. Find out how Arizona died. And don't come back here until you do.'

4

'News emerged earlier today that parents at Ellerton High School, Bishop County, are petitioning for improved security within their school. This comes after tragic events of the past year, in which four of their senior-high students lost their lives.'

This is when they talk about shutting the stable door after the horse bolted, I thought as I sat in my room watching Allyson Taylor read the evening bulletin. Our principal, Guantanamo commandant Dr Valenti, announced on camera that he had plans to boost the CCTV system around the perimeter and to carry out stop-and-search inspections on students suspected of carrying knives or guns into school. *Achtung!*

This was despite the fact that none of the four victims died on school premises. Not that this seemed to matter – like I said, most parents were sliding towards mass hysteria, afraid that every day would be their kid's last.

'Darina, are you going to eat tonight, or not?' Laura called up the stairs.

'Not,' I replied.

'Come on down. I already cooked pasta.'

'So I don't have a choice?'

'Eat!' she insisted.

Down I went, admiring Arizona's mom for the professional way she'd presented her own family tragedy on air but glad for once that I had Laura. Allyson Taylor might be well groomed, slick and classy, she might be fabulously successful and wealthy, but she was headed for divorce and she'd never been there at mealtimes to nag her kids to eat.

'Why are you smiling?' Laura asked, pushing my plate across the kitchen counter.

'Sorry, I didn't know it was against the rules.'

In the corner with his plate of pasta on one knee and his laptop on the other, Jim grunted. He meant, *Show your mom more respect, or else.*

I raised an eyebrow in his direction, meaning, *How about you show enough respect to log off and come eat at the table?*

Luckily neither of us thought it was worth open confrontation.

'Did you know Arizona Taylor had a brother with autism?' I asked Laura, casually as I could. I'd spent a long time during classes today planning my course of action and come up with the following bullet points:
* check out autism on the internet
* ask Logan to drive with me to the car repair place behind the mall
* poke around and discover more about the Taylor family reputation.

I'd done my autism research before I switched on the TV to watch Allyson read the news. I had a visit to Logan scheduled in straight after pasta. Meanwhile, maybe Laura could dish some Taylor dirt.

She paused with her fork in mid-air. 'No – I believe Arizona was an only child.'

'He would be about nine years old,' I prompted.

'When did the Taylors arrive in Ellerton? That would be eight or nine years back actually. But there was no baby that I remember.'

Wow, was Raven a well-kept secret!

Laura chewed her pasta. 'You know Arizona was Frank Taylor's daughter by his first wife? Allyson was not her birth mother.'

I shook my head. 'I didn't even know Frank was married before.'

'Yeah – also to a much younger woman. He and Allyson only married after they settled in that big new house out at Westra.' Laura was on a reminiscing roll. 'The Madisons were acquainted with them more than most at that time, so they got an invite to the wedding. Jon Madison designed their house.'

At last I thought I spotted a way through the brick wall keeping me from answers about Arizona's situation. 'So are the Madisons still friendly with the Taylors?' If so, I could call in on Summer's parents and carry out a little more investigatory activity.

Laura shook her head. 'There's a story going around that the Taylors didn't pay Jon all they owed him for his professional work so the friendship soured. And you know, Jon and Heather didn't really have too much in common with the Taylors – especially with Allyson. She runs with the media pack, and it's dog eat dog in that world.'

'So definitely no baby brother for Arizona,' I murmured. And the brick wall still stood solid.

'Allyson did take a career break around the time they were building the house,' Laura recalled. 'She switched news channels and wasn't in front of the camera for a while – my friend Kristina swore it was so she could have her face fixed, you know. When she came back on screen, I thought that Kristina was right.'

'Why? How old is Allyson Taylor?' I wanted to know.

'She's forty-seven,' Laura shot back. 'That's what I mean – she's definitely had work!'

'Not now, Darina, I'm busy.' Logan turned me down flat.

I'd walked to his place to get him to drive me to the mall, figuring that he would know his way around a car repair garage better than me. Also, he wouldn't look so out of place. Maybe he could talk to the guy in the workshop, order some parts for a car engine while I took a look around the place Arizona last recalled visiting.

But Logan said no. This was my second shock of the evening. The first had been when Jim had dropped me a comment just as I was leaving the house, right between telling me the technically correct way to load the dishwasher and heading to the fridge for a beer. 'Actually Allyson and Frank Taylor did have a baby boy,' he'd told me. 'Back then I drove a cab, for the extra income. I remember I picked Allyson and the baby up from the hospital and drove them to their new home in Westra.'

Thanks, Jim, for this small, surprise nugget. 'So how come Laura didn't know?'

He'd shrugged and pulled the tab on the can. 'I heard the baby wasn't healthy,' he'd said over the hiss of gas. 'Maybe the Taylors didn't want to talk about it with strangers.'

'Busy – how?' I challenged Logan from the porch, having stored Jim's information. I couldn't see any schoolwork spread out on the kitchen table, he didn't have his head under the hood of his car.

'I have to meet someone,' he said, picking up his car keys and swinging by.

'Someone – who?' Logan Lavelle never turned me down. He was fixated on me, close to becoming my own personal stalker.

'Just a guy,' he said, turning on the engine of his neat white Honda and driving off down the street.

So I had to wait until Wednesday afternoon for Logan to be free.

'Sure, I know the workshop,' he told me as we drove into town. 'Mike's Motors. My dad is a drinking buddy of Mike Hamill's.'

He didn't ask me why I wanted to visit, which was another change of routine for Logan.

'Don't you want to know why we're headed there?'

He signalled at the lights, taking a left down the side of the mall. 'Would I get a straight answer?'

I took a closer look at Logan's face. He felt me stare but didn't react. Sideways on, he looked more serious and mature, almost hot. I mean, he had good features and thick dark hair, a cool catch for some girl somewhere. 'I want to check it out,' I explained. 'It's the last place Arizona went before she died.'

We'd had a fight in the car, me and Logan.

'What is this – some kind of crazy mission?' he'd yelled, pulling off the road. He lost all his cool maturity and took a dive into stressed-out, I-know-best and stalker-guy role. 'First you obsess over Jonas. Then you tell me you'll never get over Phoenix. Now it's Arizona. These guys are dead, for Christ's sake!'

'I know it looks weird, Logan—'

'This is wrong, Darina. It's not healthy.'

'So let me out of the car,' I'd said calmly. I'd opened the door and continued on foot to Mike's Motors. I found it in a back lot – a workshop squeezed between a container storage yard and an awning fabrication unit. The sign looked like it needed a repaint and the broken glass panel in the door was boarded over.

'Hey!' I called.

There was no answer – just a heap of oily car innards on the concrete floor and a radio playing loud country music. The burned-out wrecks of two cars were stacked one on top of the other in a far corner. In the other I spotted Arizona's silver SUV.

I had to look twice and then a third time – the vehicle was covered in dust and half hidden behind some other stuff, but I knew Arizona's registration plate and I recognized the neat black leather interior.

'You need something?' a deep voice asked, and I spun round to see Brandon's friend Kyle Keppler.

Kyle was so not Arizona's type – the thought hit home a second time, even more clearly than before. The car technician stood with his feet wide apart, big-jawed, dirty, suspicious. *Maybe he scrubs up*, I told myself. 'Sure. I'm meeting my friend here,' I said to him.

Kyle tilted his head to one side, clearly scoring my tight jeans and T-shirt and coming up with a possible nine out of ten – not quite full marks because I had no cleavage on show. 'And his name would be?' he asked.

'Logan Lavelle.' I said the first name that came into my head. Why was Arizona's dusty SUV still in the workshop? 'We met before,' I reminded Kyle. 'You were with Brandon Rohr.'

He nodded – one quick jerk of the head. 'There's no Logan Lavelle here.'

'He didn't bring in his car for repair?'

'Take a look.'

'OK, I made a mistake. Sorry. What's with Arizona's car?

Didn't her folks want it back?' I jumped in with both feet, because why not?

Kyle frowned. 'I said, Logan's not here.'

'I hear you. I just saw the SUV – it kind of shocked me. Sorry again.'

Maybe I got through to him, or maybe he was still admiring my skinny jeans.

'No problem. Actually, Frank Taylor was happy to sell the car to my boss after Arizona . . . you know . . . passed. It needed some work.'

'Which is why she brought it here in the first place, I guess. Hey, it makes sense – you and she were an item. You work here. She'd bring it here for repair, why not?' But then she'd told me she didn't even know the name of the place, and that was clearly a lie.

Kyle's mood changed and he walked slowly and menacingly towards me. 'Did anyone tell you, your mouth could lead you into trouble?'

I backed towards the open door. 'It was only what Brandon told me. You and Arizona—'

'Brandon's full of crap,' Kyle muttered. 'What he said – it was B.S.'

Tammy Wynette was pouring her heart out on the radio. Stand by your man, or don't stand by him – I don't remember which.

I was confused and beginning to feel I'd stepped into a grimy parallel universe. 'You and Arizona, you weren't . . . ?'

Kyle took a long, last look at me. 'What do you think?' he said, slamming the workshop door behind me.

'I didn't have you down as a quitter, Darina.' My music teacher, Katie Jones, gave me a hard stare. I stood in the middle of a bunch of students who made up the music group. It included the usual suspects – Jordan, Hannah, Lucas and Logan. Around twelve of us had got together in early fall and planned a Christmas concert in memory of Summer Madison, Ellerton High's rising singing star. We missed Summer and her beautiful songs, and this would be our special way of respecting her.

'I don't have time to rehearse,' I explained. Or the focus or the desire.

'Her mind is on other things,' Logan muttered to Hannah. 'She's on her own secret mission.'

'To do what?' Scenting gossip, Hannah pricked up her ears.

'She's poking around Arizona's death. Darina's finger is on the self-destruct button, you watch.'

I blocked them out and tried to focus on my disappointed professor.

'So who do we get to replace you this late in the semester? It's really not fair of you to back out now.'

I sighed. 'You'll soon find someone who plays guitar better than me.'

'That sure won't be difficult,' Jordan murmured to Lucas.

And these are my so-called friends. On the other hand, I was dumping them big time, so I totally got where their negative reactions were coming from.

Slowly Miss Jones walked me towards the door of the music studio. 'I had you down as a fighter, not a quitter,' she said quietly. 'Are you sure you're OK?'

'As OK as anyone else around here,' I mumbled, glancing over my shoulder to see Logan deep in gossip with my on–off buddy, Hannah Stoltmann.

Was I right to quit the concert? I went home and brooded.

This was already Friday, and since my visit to Mike's Motors had misfired, I was way down in the depths of despair. *I can't hack this Arizona stuff!* ran through my head like a funeral dirge. *I don't know what else I can do!*

Friday evening was Laura and Jim's night at the movies so I had the house to myself. I skipped supper and checked out autism sites one more time. *Autism disorder – Infantile autism – Fragile X syndrome – epilepsy.* I read that kids born with autism have feeding difficulties and they never smile. They can rock back and forth in a chair and stare at their hands all day. This can happen to between three and six babies in every hundred, or to 8.7 in every thousand, depending on which site you read. It may be down to rubella during the first trimester of pregnancy or to wrong levels of serotonin in the brain – who really knows? Anyway, this was over my head so I skipped these parts.

What I was interested in were the autistic kids with an outstanding ability – maybe ten per cent of sufferers. They may have amazing rote memory or musical ability, and there's one famous case in the UK where the kid could take one glance at a building – their Houses of Parliament or our White House, say – put pencil to paper and reproduce the whole thing from memory. In the end, this kid's artwork got famous. *They could be talking about Raven!* I thought.

Mostly though, autism can be pure misery. No smiles, no speech. These kids don't look you in the eye, and because there may be other severe mental health issues they can be on a stack of medication their whole lives.

So what do you do when life deals you a hand like that? I stopped scrolling with the mouse and tried to imagine how the Taylors had coped after Allyson took him home in Jim's cab. Arizona had talked about diagnoses and treatments, hospitals and schools. She'd also said her parents didn't want to believe it had happened.

'I heard the baby wasn't healthy,' Jim had told me. It turned out he was right and the parents had fallen into denial, as in: *Let's keep the illness a secret and then maybe the problem will go away.*

Was I right? I would ask Arizona next time we met.

The thought took me away from my laptop to my bedroom window. I stared out at the clear sky. *When will next time be?* Not until I'd found the facts behind the myth of Arizona's suicide – Hunter had made that crystal clear. I closed my eyes and pictured the overlord's strong, severe features, the faded angel-wing tattoo on his forehead. And I remembered the story Phoenix had told about Hunter being shot through the temple at close range by the man who had just attempted to rape his wife, Marie.

I'm dying here! I told the millions of stars. *I need to go up to Foxton Ridge, to find Phoenix and check he's still there.*

'Give me one reason why I don't send you back to limbo – and this time for good.' Or words to that effect. It was Hunter again – folding his arms astride the patch of burned ground, his anger close to the surface. Even the memory of it scared me – the way the anger could blaze up and wipe out anyone in its path. Hunter was overlord and he had absolute power to hypnotize, read minds, even, as a total last resort, to call those lost souls down to beat their wings and travel with him through time to the beginning or end of the world and beyond.

I trembled at the memory of my own time travel experience to nail down Matt Fortune as Jonas's killer, how I never felt such pain before and came back traumatized and exhausted. Which is why Hunter only did it after every other method had failed.

Overlord. Ruler of everything: All-powerful Hunter.

Through the open window I felt a breath of cool breeze. The white drapes fluttered. When I turned around, Phoenix was standing in the room.

'Oh, thank God!' I flung myself into his arms, gripping the sleeves of his jacket, my head against his shoulder. 'I didn't know – I was scared that . . .'

'Me too.' He held me tight, pressing his lips against the top of my head.

'So scared,' I breathed. 'I didn't dare come back to Foxton. Is Hunter still mad with us?'

'He's been in a mean mood. He sent me and Lee up to Government Bridge to stand watch.'

'That's harsh.' Knowing the jealous feelings Phoenix had about Lee, knowing that Hunter would see the dynamics all too clearly. 'He certainly figured out how to hurt us.'

'We were up there twenty-four seven.' Phoenix let go of me and stood back so he could see my face. 'I feel so bad, Darina. Lee's new to this, but he's able to read my thoughts pretty clearly. He saw what a crazy idiot I'd been.'

I managed a small grin. 'Did he beat you up over it?'

'No, he was cool. He told me, if you'd been his girl, he'd have reacted the same way.'

'So I don't need to worry about two Beautiful Dead guys fighting over me?'

'Lee's cool,' Phoenix insisted. He slid his arm around my waist and sat me on the bed beside him. 'Have you any idea how low the temperature drops out there late at night?'

'Now I'm crying for you!'

'You should be.'

We stopped talking and made up for all the full-on kisses we'd missed out on lately. I fell into the moment, loving the pressure of his lips on mine, then on my cheeks and softly on my eyelids, deep in that floaty, unreal feeling you get . . . when Phoenix slowly leaned back. 'You know something?'

'No – what?'

'Those contractors at Government Bridge – they're not even there any more. It turns out the surveyor's new report said there was no need to strengthen the bridge after all.'

'All those nights out in the cold!' I laughed. This time our kisses were light-hearted: smile – kiss – smile – pucker lips for another kiss. 'And I bet Hunter knew that would happen – he was the one who played around with the surveyor's mental state, remember.'

Talking of mental states, I kept from puckering up long enough to tell Phoenix what I'd found out about Raven Taylor's illness, plus how I'd been along to Mike's Motors, spotted Arizona's SUV and got booted out by Kyle Keppler. 'So much weird stuff,' I said with a shake of my head. 'Arizona told me she didn't even know the name of the car repair place, but it turns out that's where her boyfriend works!'

Phoenix stretched out his legs and lay back on the bed. 'You want to know something else?'

I snuggled beside him, resting my arm across his chest. 'Do I? The truth is, I wouldn't care if we didn't talk too much right now.'

He cupped his hand over my mouth and made me listen. 'It was earlier tonight – Hunter let me and Lee off the hook and said we could go back to the barn to rest up. That was OK by me. The first person I saw when I got back was Arizona. She was out in the meadow, standing under the moon and stars, not looking at anything, not listening, like she wasn't really there. She heard me but she didn't turn to look.'

'You think she was angry?' Maybe with me for failing to move forward.

'Not angry,' Phoenix murmured. 'More sad.'

'Sad?' I didn't connect the emotion with the Arizona I knew. 'Tears and all?'

He gave a low laugh. 'We don't do tears.'

'Oh.' The Beautiful Dead didn't do heartbeats either. They were bloodless, cold and pale, and now I knew they couldn't weep either. 'Did you tune in and read what was going on inside her head?'

He propped himself against my pillow and shrugged. 'Arizona's powers are strong,' he admitted. 'But until tonight in the meadow I didn't know how way ahead of me she is. I mean, I tried to tune in but there was a force there stopping me.'

'She blocked you so you couldn't do your telepathy thing?' I guessed this was totally against the rules and wondered what Hunter would say.

'So then I reached out. I wanted to tell her it was OK, she wasn't in any danger, but she pushed me away and told me that yes she was in danger, and I should go ask Hunter about it.'

'So you did?' The story was getting through to me. I thought of Arizona standing cold and alone in the meadow, of her pushing Phoenix away.

'OK, this is the really weird part. I found Hunter in the house, up in the bedroom, sitting with his head in his hands, ignoring me. I waited until he was ready to look up. He asked me, "Phoenix, did anyone ever betray you?" and I said no, not that I know about.'

Phoenix's low voice ceased. I waited.

'If it was possible, I'd say the guy had aged,' he went on. 'He stooped under a heavy weight; he looked confused.'

'This is Hunter we're talking about?' I checked.

'It turns out he'd had a confrontation with Arizona.'

'Wow. The girl's either brave or crazy.'

'Hunter spelled it out to me. Arizona had accused him of not working hard enough to sort out her mess. She'd told him no way would you break through the walls of silence out there without more help.'

'She challenged the overlord?' This didn't happen – ever! I was amazed Arizona was still here on the far side.

'Worse. She said, how come he was so sure he was right? Didn't it occur to him that things didn't always happen the way he saw them?'

'And Hunter told you this?'

'Yeah. Arizona must have been crazy by this point, because she asked him was he sure about the way he died, defending his wife? Was it possible that Marie hadn't been fighting off her attacker, that she'd actually betrayed him with the guy . . .'

'Peter Mentone.'

I already mentioned part of this story. To recap – way back at the beginning of the twentieth century, Mentone was Hunter and Marie's nearest neighbour. He'd called when Hunter was out. Hunter had got back early and discovered the two of them together.

'You can't say that to Hunter!' I gasped. The shock made me sit up.

'Arizona did,' Phoenix insisted. 'You think the guy's made of steel, but you should've seen the way he looked when I walked into the room. He was a broken man. That's why he asked me the stuff about betrayal. And then he stood up and tried to shake it off. He said he had something he wanted me to do.'

'I thought you were supposed to rest up?'

'He changed his mind. He said I had to bring you up to Foxton right away.'

My heart gave a leap – Phoenix was here to take me

back with him. I got ready to leave.

Phoenix made me wait. He hadn't finished what he had to tell me. 'Only, Hunter didn't say, "Fetch Darina", he said, "Fetch Marie".'

I gasped. Why did this slip of the tongue make me tremble and send a shiver down my spine?

'Summer says you look like Marie, remember.' Phoenix took my hand and led me to the window. 'She saw the old photograph.'

'Don't. This messes with my head. In any case, you knew what he meant, so here you are – to fetch me. Did he tell you why?'

'Because of Arizona,' Phoenix explained. 'There's more stuff she's not been saying. Hunter found out she's been holding out on us big time.'

I wasn't so shocked by the revelation as Phoenix thought I would be.

So now Hunter and the Beautiful Dead knew what I'd felt all along – that Arizona hid important truths for her own reasons. In other words, she was one of them but you couldn't always trust her.

'So now you know,' I told Phoenix as he got ready to dematerialize me. 'And now I'm not fighting a lone battle – Hunter will force the truth out of her, won't he?'

'I have no idea. This is new territory,' he admitted. 'OK,

Darina – Hunter needs you there sooner than we could get in your car and drive out, so we do it the Beautiful Dead way.'

'I'm ready!' This was also new – me getting to travel through space their way – and I was definitely eager to experience it.

'It won't hurt,' Phoenix promised. 'Just remember – don't let go of me.'

I nodded, excited by the beating wings that had descended around us, raising the light silk drapes in a flurry of activity. They caused a breeze that sucked the fabric out through the open window.

Phoenix faced me and took both my hands. 'Close your eyes,' he murmured, 'and don't open them again until I tell you.'

I did this, a little nervous now that the wings beat louder and their energy was more threatening. 'I'm holding tight,' I promised, scared too by the moving patterns imprinted on the inner side of my eyelids – zig-zags and darting shafts of orange and purple. 'How long does this take?'

Phoenix didn't answer. He kept hold of me amidst the wings and the weird shapes, his hands cool but steady. I felt a strong wind, cold as death, a dizzy, floating sensation, almost as if my brain was loose inside my skull

– totally disorientating – and finally a bright white light penetrating my closed lids.

'OK, open your eyes,' Phoenix said at last.

We were in the barn below Foxton Ridge. It was dark and there were no oil lamps, only slender shafts of moonlight falling across the floor.

'Crazy!' I kept hold of Phoenix's hands until I found my balance and was able to look around. 'So where is everyone?'

We walked outside, where it was still pitch black. There was a light on in the house, so we walked across.

'Hey.' Iceman heard our footsteps and opened the door. He smiled at me. 'Are you OK, Darina?'

'That was so weird,' I told him. 'But yeah, I'm cool.'

Phoenix stepped inside the house ahead of me. 'Where's Arizona?' he asked.

'Gone.'

'Gone where?' Iceman's answer shocked me. I thought he meant she'd finally angered Hunter so much with her attitude that he'd sent her away from the far side for good.

'No one knows. Wherever she went, Hunter took her. He said for you two to wait here.'

'How long will he be?' Phoenix had told me he had to get me out to Foxton in a hurry – hence the magic trip.

Now it seemed that something even more important had come up.

'As long as it takes.' Iceman sighed and turned to Phoenix. 'I never saw Hunter act this way before.'

Phoenix nodded. 'I never saw anyone *disobey* him before.'

'Yeah, you did,' I reminded him. 'We overstepped the mark on Monday night, remember. But I guess that was nothing compared with Arizona.'

'In any case, we wait,' Phoenix sat on the edge of the table, his long legs stretched towards the stove. 'Sit,' he told me, pointing towards the rocking-chair. 'Try and get some sleep.'

'No way,' I replied, sitting anyway. 'I'm way too wired for that.'

Six hours later, Phoenix woke me with a kiss.

'Do that again,' I whispered. 'Or I'll think I'm still dreaming.'

He kissed my lips softly, then the side of my neck. 'Still no sign of Hunter and Arizona,' he reported. 'But come and take a look at this.'

I followed him out of the house to a world still in black shadow, with only the molten gold rim of the sun showing on the horizon. We watched it rise, faster than you would believe, turning the sky a crazy orange, lightening to pink and spilling itself over the jagged mountains.

'Cool, huh?' Phoenix whispered in my ear.

'I have no words,' I told him. Right that moment, life was too perfect.

The silence was broken by Summer running down the hillside and across the meadow. She was a fantasy girl – golden-haired, long-limbed, beautiful. 'There are horse riders up by Angel Rock,' she reported urgently. 'I think maybe they rode out early to see the dawn.'

Her voice brought Donna and Lee across the yard. 'Let's go,' Donna said before I had time to react. 'Darina, maybe you should stay here.'

Quickly the four of them set off in the direction Summer had come from, leaving me dumb and standing on the porch.

Since when did I take orders from Donna? I asked myself, setting off at half their pace, but keeping them within my sights. The sun was up and I knew my own way to Angel Rock.

Phoenix, Summer, Donna and Lee soon vanished over the ridge. I struggled on after them, making the stand of aspens and the water tower in time to see a horse trailer parked at the end of a dirt track and three riders in the distance.

The four Beautiful Dead had spread out across the next hillside. Then I felt the familiar breeze sweep down from Amos Peak, pressing the long grass flat, sighing across the landscape.

The horses heard it too. What was it – wind or wings? Where did it come from?

This is going to spook them big time, I realized. I saw Donna and Lee disappear from sight around the back of the granite formation they call Angel Rock, heard the wings beat louder and felt the bright dawn light begin to fade back into shadow.

Now the three riders struggled to keep their horses under control. They turned their backs to the gusts, only to find that the wind had changed direction and was swirling their horses' manes and tails every which way. One horse – a brown and white Paint – reared on to its hind legs.

I was still too far away to see or hear the details. The wings beat and raised a force field which terrified the horses. They wanted to be out of there, but their terrified riders pulled hard on the reins. 'Stop!' I called to Phoenix.

He heard me and yelled at Summer, who nodded and backed off down the hillside. Phoenix too hung back. But Lee and Donna were operating separately, and they were pressing in on the horses and riders, driving them away from the barn and house, further into the Amos wilderness of rocks and thorn bush. 'Phoenix, tell them to stop!' I called again.

It was too late. The rider of the Paint lost her reins and her horse took off. The second horse, an Appaloosa, bucked and kicked out. Its rider fell forward against its neck and let it gallop after the first. Which left the third sorrel horse stranded by Angel Rock with the pulsating wind in its ears and nostrils, making it whinny in terror.

I saw the horse swing around suddenly and the rider fall sideways in the saddle. The mare reared, the rider was thrown backwards. She struggled to get back and there was a moment when I thought she would make it, but no – her balance was too far gone and she was thrown to the ground. Free at last, the horse bolted.

Summer and Phoenix ran to the fallen rider. I caught up with them as they bent over her and found she was alive but unconscious. She lay on a flat ledge of rock, one arm crooked behind her back, her eyes shut.

'My God, what do we do?' I gasped.

Lee and Donna were still raising the force field of terror from behind Angel Rock, the wind was still driving down the slope. In the distance, the riders and horses ran out of control.

'Don't move her,' I warned Summer. 'Not until

we know if she broke any bones.'

'Go and make Lee and Donna quit,' Phoenix told her. He stayed with me to check the woman's pulse. Then I leaned in close and felt her warm breath against my cheek.

'It looks like her arm's broken. What were you thinking back there? You don't do your beating wings thing when there are horses involved.'

'It ran out of control,' Phoenix admitted. He stepped back as the woman's eyelids began to flutter. 'She's waking up.'

'You four need to get out of here fast,' I decided. 'Grab the others – go!'

I watched her eyes flicker open, heard her groan. 'Go, Phoenix!'

So he gathered Summer, Donna and Lee, and they got out of sight before the injured rider knew where she was.

'It's OK,' I told her as she raised herself on one elbow. Now I got to take a closer look I saw she wasn't young – maybe in her fifties. Her dark hair, twisted back into a braid, was threaded with grey, her face was lined, but she was still slender and in good shape.

'I don't know what happened,' she told me in a faint voice. 'My horse spooked. There was a weird kind of wind – was it a hurricane?'

'Don't talk, you don't have to worry – I'll get you out of here.'

As she tried to ease her right arm, she groaned. Then she lay back on the ledge, tears leaking from the corners of her eyes.

'I guess the arm's broken,' I confirmed. 'You don't hurt anywhere else?'

The woman shook her head. 'I have to get to a hospital,' she sighed.

'I know. Lie still, don't try to move. I have to see if I can get a signal on my cell.'

Taking the phone from my jeans pocket, I called 911. *Call Failed* – once . . . twice . . . three times. I tried again – at last it rang through.

'We need paramedics up by Foxton Ridge,' I told the operator. 'I have a woman with injuries. She took a fall from her horse. The exact location is Angel Rock. You guys need to get here fast as you can.'

I got it in the neck from all sides.

'I can't believe you did this to me!' Laura wailed. 'Jim and I arrive back from the movies and go to bed thinking you're safe in your room. It turns out your bed wasn't even slept in!'

'So how come you were up at Angel Rock at dawn?' Logan wanted to know after Laura had made a frantic call and he spoke to me on the phone. 'No, don't tell me. I really don't want to know.'

Before that, I was under serious pressure from the paramedics. 'Did you see what caused the accident? What happened to spook the horses? Was there anybody else at the scene?'

And the doctors in the hospital. 'You're saying you drove out there alone?' I'd lied about this, naturally. 'Did your parents know where you were?'

Next time someone gets thrown from a horse I'll cross the road and walk on by, I thought.

I left the hospital around eleven and hitched a ride with an off-duty medic. I got home a couple of hours later, trying to come up with an excuse that would satisfy Laura.

'I couldn't sleep so I got up early.'

'Your bed!' she yelled, eyes bulging, fists clenched. 'You didn't even lie on it.'

I closed my eyes and shook my head. 'Please,' I begged.

'Where did you go?' she stampeded on. 'I didn't hear you leave. I would've heard you start the car.'

'Don't turn your back on your mother,' Jim warned. 'And try telling us the truth for once in your life.'

That was it – enough! 'Quit telling me what to do,' I yelled back at him. I acknowledged the elephant that was always in the room. 'You have no right. You're not even my dad!'

You'd think that I'd socked Laura in the stomach, the way she gasped and flopped down on the couch. She was still in her nightwear, her pink towelling gown wrapped around her. The mascara from last night was smudged down her pale cheeks.

Jim cocked his head to one side, his eyes narrow and glittering. 'I didn't hear you say that, Darina.'

'Whatever!' It was time to flounce out, I didn't care where.

I was out of there, turning the ignition in my car when Logan's Honda pulled across the driveway, blocking me in. 'Get out of my way!' I yelled.

He slammed his car door and strode up the drive. 'Stop screaming at me. You're not going any place.'

I jumped out, cutting across the patch of grass and jumping the low fence on to the sidewalk. 'Back off, Logan.' The guy was too much. 'You told me on the phone – you don't want to know!'

Logan refused to be shaken off. We were running down the street, he was grabbing me by the arm. 'You're out of line, you hear?'

Elephant time again. 'Logan, you're worse than Jim. You totally don't have any right to force your opinion on me. You're nothing in my life – OK?'

And Logan's turn to be socked senseless. He drew a sharp breath and stepped into the gutter.

I was free to run on but I stopped to drive the point home. 'You're not my brother or my boyfriend or my father, you're my . . . no, you're not *even* my friend!' I couldn't have hurt him more if I'd tried.

I was shocked – instead of staying down under the knockout punch the way Laura and Jim had done, Logan came back at me. He could sprint faster than me too. So there he was, blocking my way again.

'Truth time?' he said, his voice dry and harsh. 'You want to hear it the way it is, Darina? You're acting like a total screwball. No one can believe a word you say. Nobody – not Hannah, not Lucas – nobody likes you, the way you're acting.'

'Run that by me again,' I argued, my chest heaving. 'Didn't I just rescue an injured woman from off the side of a mountain? Since when was that a crime?'

'That's not the point and you know it. What's the big thing with Angel Rock and Foxton? What are you hiding? What takes you out there before dawn?'

'No comment!'

I succeeded in pushing past him at last. We hit a line of maple trees, I heard the rustling leaves build to the sound of wings beating.

'This is a free country, Logan. I can go where I like.'

'So go,' he said, suddenly resigned. He'd gone the distance, reached the final bell with me. The fight was over and in the end the referee would call it, whoever that would be.

I circled him warily, still expecting him to land a rabbit punch. 'So you'll move your car?' I checked.

'Sure.' He shrugged and walked back the way we came.

'Go wherever it is you need to go, Darina. But from now on, don't come to my house looking for help the next time you reach rock bottom and you need a shoulder to cry on.'

As it happened, even though Logan cleared my exit, I still couldn't drive away.

'Darina, you have a visitor,' Jim told me from the porch before I could ease into gear.

There was a stranger holding a bunch of flowers standing next to him and it took me some time to remember where I'd seen him before. It didn't click until he stepped out of the shadows and I made out his skinny frame and slicked-back grey hair. It was the gardener guy from the Taylors' place. Anyone else, and I would have made my excuses and left.

Peter the gardener recognized me at about the same moment. I saw him blink and swallow. Then he kept on coming down the drive. 'Peter Hall,' he introduced himself through the driver's window. 'I came to say thanks.'

'For what?' I was thinking along the lines of Raven Taylor and the screwed-up drawing and the kid's scared eyes.

'For bringing my wife, Jenna, off the mountain

earlier today. Without you, the incident could have turned nasty.'

We went into the house. Laura put the lilies in a vase, then she and Jim left me alone to speak with Peter.

'I had no idea she was your wife,' I told him.

'Thank you anyway,' he told me. 'I just came from the hospital. The doctors want to keep her there for a couple of days. They need to wait until the trauma subsides before they decide what to do next – maybe surgery, maybe not. Plus, Jenna's pretty shaken up so they sedated her.'

'She's going to be OK?' I asked.

'Sure. She wanted me to say thanks.'

'It's weird that we already met,' I reminded him.

He chose not to follow this up. 'I have to go. I need to pick up Jenna's horse trailer from Foxton.' Peter Hall cut the conversation short by getting up to leave. 'So thank you, Darina.'

I followed him out of the house, glad anyway to be out of Laura's hearing. 'What took your wife and her riding buddies up there so early?' I asked.

'Some romantic notion about watching the sun come up over Amos Peak. They've been planning to do it all fall.'

'And look what happens when they do,' I sighed. 'Do

they know what spooked Jenna's horse?'

'No clue,' Peter told me, heading for his truck which was parked further down the street. 'They say horses can see in the dark, so maybe they noticed something in the shadow of a rock – coyote maybe. And the guy who was riding with them said there was a weird wind up there – horses hate squally weather, it drives them crazy.'

'Yeah, I guess that was it.' Relieved, standing between him and his vehicle, I still had a long list of questions, not all connected with this morning's rescue. 'Do you want me to show you exactly where they parked the trailer?' I asked.

'No – thanks. You've already helped plenty.'

'Really – it's no problem. I'd like to.'

'Jump in then,' he told me, not wanting to be impolite. Peter Hall was a well-brought-up guy, bringing home-grown lilies to say thank you and speaking with an educated accent. 'Do you need to tell your folks?' he asked.

I shook my head and climbed in the passenger side. 'Did you pick the flowers from the Taylors' garden?' I asked. 'Only, I remember seeing pink lilies by their summer house.'

'No, these were from my place. Jenna likes to grow flowers. Do I turn left out of town?'

'At the next lights. Head for Turkey Shoot Ridge.

How long have you worked for the Taylors?'

'Several years. Why?'

'No reason.' I sat quiet as we cruised out of town, past a small industrial park, through some run-down housing into the burn-out area. We hit the highway at around three-thirty in the afternoon.

It's time I ran into some luck. I thought, with Peter's radio playing quietly in the background. If you could call it luck that a woman falls from her horse and brings me into contact with the one guy I *know* gets up close and personal with Raven Taylor.

'So, Darina, are you a student at Ellerton High?' Peter asked me as we settled into our journey.

I nodded.

'And can I ask what brought you out to Foxton early today?'

I gave the old 'couldn't sleep' excuse. 'I like to drive,' I explained. 'I get in the car and try to get rid of my demons.'

Peter nodded like he understood. 'Lucky for Jenna you did.'

'You ought to know – I knew Arizona,' I told him quietly, jumping right in.

The radio gave us tomorrow's weather forecast. Peter Hall glanced at me. 'It's almost a year now,' he said quietly. 'There was Jonas before her, and Summer and Phoenix since.'

Slight and skinny, wearing dark-blue jeans and a crisp pale-blue shirt – the slim hands on the steering wheel didn't look like they'd spent forty years plus doing hard physical work. These were some of the things about him that didn't add up.

'The families are hit hard,' I commented. 'Mrs Madison doesn't leave the house much. And I saw Jonas's mom at Bob's wake. It's real bad for them.'

'I've been with the Taylors a long time,' he informed me. We'd driven past the giant neon crucifix on the hill – a marker I used every time I drove this road. We were ten minutes from the Foxton turn off. 'I miss that girl more than I can say.'

'You do? I mean, sure you do.' I tried to keep the surprise out of my voice, but Peter picked it up.

'She was a complex kid – hard to get to know,' he went on. 'But once you saw what went on behind that slick image she built up, she won you right over to her side.'

'I never knew her well,' I admitted. Slowly, slowly I was turning the key and behind that door lay the real Arizona Taylor. 'I don't know anyone who did.'

'Hard on the outside, soft as honey on the inside. A sweet, sweet girl.'

'Turn left at the lights,' I told him, swallowing my surprise as we came to the Foxton junction. 'Drive by the creek, past the fishermen's shacks.'

'You should've seen her take care of Raven,' Peter explained. 'She loved him like no one else did. The others – Frank and Allyson – they don't have the patience or the time. They don't have the heart. But Arizona did.'

I shook my head in disbelief. 'So we can talk about Raven?'

'Sure. You saw him in the summer house. What's the use pretending you didn't?'

'I just thought—'

'No one speaks about Raven, huh? That's the way his parents want to play it.'

'And Arizona, when she was alive – the same?'

He nodded. 'The entire family. With Frank and Allyson, it's out of some kind of shame, like he's a black mark against their name. That's mostly why they send him to residential school. But Arizona had different reasons – she thought silence was the best way to protect him. She didn't want people asking questions, upsetting him in that way.'

'And where do you come in?'

'I'm the part-time gardener,' he shot back.

'And bodyguard?'

'Gardener – period.' The track was getting rough, we came to a sharp bend and he put on the brakes. The back wheels spat up dirt. 'That is, until my contract with them runs out at the end of this month.'

'Then what?'

'Then the house gets sold and I lose my job.'

'Here's the horse trailer,' I said, 'right up ahead.'

I helped Peter hitch the trailer on to his truck, letting time pass before I pried some more. I decided I liked the guy – he was solid and straightforward, he didn't play mind games.

He put me in the driving seat of his truck and told me to reverse towards the trailer. 'OK, hold it there. I'm turning the lever – that's cool. Good, we're hitched. Want to drive?' he asked when he walked back to the truck.

'I never towed a trailer before,' I admitted.

'You look like you can handle it,' he told me with a grin. He jumped in the passenger side and advised me on the best way to ease forward on to the track. 'So did you get what you wanted out of your visit with Frank?'

'No. I asked for music lessons but he turned me down.' I drove slowly along the creek side towards the main highway. 'Actually, I didn't want to learn guitar,' I confessed. 'I'd heard stories about Arizona. I wanted to check them out.'

'What kind of stories?' For a second Peter's defences were back up.

'Some people are saying she didn't commit suicide out at Hartmann. That wasn't how it happened.' Was that a step too far? Would the hired help totally clam up?

But no.

'I agree with them,' he told me with a ton of emotion behind his words. 'What reason did Arizona have to take her own life? Why in God's name would she leave Raven behind?'

'Exactly!' In my excitement I pressed the gas pedal instead of the brake and we shot the junction on to the freeway. Luckily the lights were green.

'She looked out for him,' Frank insisted. 'To tell you the truth, she was a better mother to the boy than Allyson ever was.'

'Too interested in her career, huh?' I was back in control, coasting down towards Turkey Shoot.

'Not really that. A lot of women have careers and a family, no problem. No – with Allyson it's like she has no maternal instinct. It's a missing gene.'

'Frank Taylor doesn't come across as a warm, loving kind of guy either.' He was all brain and no heart, it seemed to me.

'Now you understand why Arizona stepped into the

parenting role. And Jenna and I – we did what we could. Still do, as long as we're able.'

I drove in silence for a while. A new question had wormed itself into my brain, but I shelved it for a while. 'What is it with Raven?' I asked instead. 'OK, so he has autism and they feel ashamed. But what's the bottom line – why do they really hide him away?'

'He needs a lot of care – medication and supervision twenty-four seven. Then there are his mood swings which can lead to self-harm. Plus, he suffers from hyperactivity. The only time he's calm is when he's drawing.'

'That sounds tough to handle. And does he understand much of what goes on around him? Can he talk?' Arizona had told me he didn't even know what a smile meant, remember.

'No speech,' Peter confirmed. 'But Arizona had a way of getting through to him. She was the only one who could.'

'He really misses her?'

'Like crazy. When he's home from school, he walks from room to room, looking for her, wanting to show her his latest sketches.'

'And you?' There – the question slithered out. 'Arizona meant more to you than you're telling me?'

Peter took a deep breath, overcame whatever doubts were still lingering and forged ahead. 'Jenna and I – we're the parents of Frank's first wife, Kathryn.'

'You're Arizona's grandparents?' I gasped.

'It was tragic – Kathryn died giving birth to Arizona. She never knew her mother, so we did all we could to fill the gap.'

'I warned you she was too clever for you.' Hunter was himself again, stern and in control. He'd heard me coming after Peter had dropped me off at my house, where I'd picked up my car and headed straight back out to Foxton. The overlord had walked out of the barn to meet me.

'What you said was "subtle", not clever. I don't call her lying and concealing a clever thing to do. Guess the latest – she has grandparents!'

He looked carefully at me. 'You're angry.'

'Of course I'm angry. Aren't you?' In fact, I half expected this to be my last discussion about Arizona with the leader of the Beautiful Dead. 'Tell me – is she out of here? Did you send her back to limbo?'

'Which answer do you want – yes or no?'

'Yes, if she carries on lying to us. If it was down to me, I'd say goodbye, Arizona and move on to Summer.' Only there was Raven's future in the balance, and the remote chance that I could find out the truth about what happened to his sister and get him to understand.

'Exactly.' Hunter read my thoughts. 'That's why we're here.'

'So you didn't send her back, even after what she did?' It was cold out here in the yard, and for once the moon was behind a dense bank of clouds. I shivered as I waited impatiently for Hunter's answer.

'I dealt with that,' he said slowly. 'From now on Arizona will be honest.'

'She'd better be, because I've got a lot of new stuff on her. For instance, these grandparents, Jenna and Peter Hall – they care about Raven. Arizona isn't the only one looking out for him.'

'But Arizona heard they're leaving at the end of the month.' Hunter and Arizona were ahead of me, as always. 'They're not blood relatives to Raven. Allyson Taylor won't grant them the right to carry on visiting.'

'Arizona told you that?'

He nodded. 'Since I last saw you, we reached a better understanding.'

'You forgave her?' For holding out, for challenging his authority, for casting a shadow of doubt over the actions of his long-dead wife. I was stunned but I got my head together and pressed on. 'Did she say why she concealed all that stuff?'

He scratched his jaw. 'You have to admire her strength of mind,' he said without answering my question. 'She kept up that barrier for almost a year, even with me. No one got through it. That shows character.'

'But *why*?'

'Here she is,' Hunter said, stepping to one side so I could see Arizona in silhouette, standing in the barn doorway, backed by soft lamplight. 'You can ask her yourself.'

'I'm shocked Hunter didn't punish you,' I told Arizona as we walked the dark hillside.

'What makes you think I'm not punished?' She was slightly ahead of me, dressed in only a T-shirt and jeans. The wind blew her hair across her face.

'You're still here,' I pointed out.

'He cut back my time on the far side,' she said in a flat voice. 'I had two weeks, now I only have one.'

'Jeez!' I caught up with her so I could make out the expression on her face. 'Seven days to sort out the whole lousy mess.'

'Plus, he sent me back to the day it happened – to try and make me remember more details. It hurt like hell.'

'Don't I know it? So he actually time travelled you. Did it work?'

Arizona shook her head. 'I got to the point on the day

I died where I was walking by the lake. I can still see that in my head – the low sun, the frost on the shore, the sparkling water. I wasn't alone, but I don't know who was with me, and I was scared.'

'Then what?'

'Then there was a blast of fear – pure terror – a blur then a total blank. Hunter pulled me out of there and dragged me back to the present. It felt like I was being torn apart. And all for nothing.'

We walked a while, keeping step. 'I guess Hunter knew that there'd be nothing new.'

'Like I say, he was punishing me. I relived it to a certain point, and for what?'

'For the chance to have this conversation with me,' I pointed out. 'It's truth time, Arizona, and I'm all ears.'

We sat under the water tower, leaning against its iron legs and surrounded by silence. I waited a long time for Arizona to begin.

'Picture this. It seems like all my life I'm living in a house with people who are in total denial. At first they pretend nothing is wrong with their darling baby boy. Raven won't feed and he won't hold eye contact, but why worry? The au pair deals with the feeding problem while Dad and Allyson go to work. Raven has seizures – they call in the doctors, who convince them he'll grow out of it. They call it *petit mal*, so it sounds fancy and everything's OK.'

'You knew it wasn't?'

'From the very start. He was only a small baby when I first watched him dig his nails into his own flesh. When he got teeth, he bit himself instead. He was so little and helpless. We both were.'

'I'm sorry.'

'Don't be. I soon toughened up. I got to understand that helpless wasn't a good place to be, so I began to throw in challenges – "How come you're not picking up on this? Why don't you make some real effort here?" But my dad and Allyson, they don't do illness and disability.'

I broke in to tell her that I had, as a matter of fact, learned a lot of this from her grandfather. If she was shocked or ashamed, she hid it well. 'You were a kid back then,' I pointed out. 'But Peter and Jenna – they were adults. They could see what was happening – surely they cared.'

Arizona gave me one of her hard, dismissive glances. '*Everybody* cared,' she argued. 'But Allyson – she's the powerful one. She did things her way. She said if my grandparents had any complaints about the way she was handling Raven's situation, they could leave.'

'Scary lady!'

'Archetypal wicked stepmother. And I was in her way.'

'I get that,' I muttered. (For Allyson in Arizona's situation, read Jim in mine.)

'So they packaged up Raven's condition with more fancy labels. One morning I woke up and he was gone.'

'Away to school?'

'Allyson was busy reading the news on TV, my dad was in Europe at a conference. That left the home-help to tell me the name of the school where they'd taken my brother – the Lindsey Institute. She said he'd be back – eventually.'

'Ouch. Peter said you were the only one who knew how to get through to Raven. How did you do that?'

'I focused on what he's good at,' she explained, as if the answer was plain for anyone to see. 'He likes drawing.'

'So you drew?'

'Yeah, and I showed him pictures – sometimes photographs, sometimes paintings. There's a big art gallery in the city – I took him there. He likes Andy Warhol – the way he repeats silk-screen images over and over. Marilyn Monroe. Elizabeth Taylor. The soup cans.'

'I'll remember that,' I promised, shocked when my comment brought tears to her eyes. 'When this is over, I'll take him to see the Andy Warhols.'

Arizona broke down and cried. 'Without me there to

protect him, they'll lock him up and throw away the key,' she wept. 'After the divorce, I know that's what they'll do!'

'Look,' I said, pulling Raven's crumpled drawing from my pocket. I'd kept it there as the one concrete thing to hang on to. I unfolded it and gave it to her.

Her hands trembled as she studied every line of the sketch. 'Thank you,' she whispered over and over. 'Oh, Raven, poor baby. What's going to happen now?'

When the going is tough, you grow a tough shell to help you deal with it – that's what I'd learned these last few hours. But then the drawing of a house on a screwed-up piece of paper makes a crack in the shell and the light pours in. I saw a new Arizona – one I wanted to help at last.

'So you have to tell me about Kyle Keppler,' I insisted as we walked under the aspens on Foxton Ridge. 'What do I need to know?'

She veered off the top of the ridge, down the dark side of the hill. 'It's complicated.'

'How complicated? Listen – you told me you didn't know the name of Mike Hamill's repair shop, yet that's where your boyfriend works. So how come you kept that from me?'

'I didn't want Kyle to be implicated.'

'Officially he isn't, so you did a good job,' I muttered.

'And by the way, did you know that he's now denying you were ever his girl?' This obviously hurt her and I was sorry. 'Your car is still in the workshop, so I was able to figure out a few things for myself.'

'That I did take it in for repair that day? That, afterwards, my dad and Allyson didn't care enough to want it back? Also, they hid all the photos and sent my clothes to the charity store. What else?'

'Both you and Kyle were covering up – I don't know what. Anyway, why did you need to keep his name out of it?'

'Because what we had – our relationship – was a secret.'

'Brandon Rohr knew,' I told her. '*He* told me.'

Arizona slowed down, wrapped her hand around a slender tree trunk and gazed up at the dark canopy. 'Brandon swore to Kyle that he wouldn't. Kyle's his buddy, he trusted him.'

'Mistake! Even I don't trust Brandon, and he's Phoenix's brother, for Christ's sake. He dances to his own beat.'

Arizona swung around the tree trunk and we came face to face. 'Go ahead, give me some reasons why I wouldn't want people to know about me and Kyle.'

'*Numero uno* – he's so not your type.'

'Wrong side of the tracks?'

I nodded. 'Plus, he's prehistoric.'

125

'Twenty-two,' she confirmed. 'And?'

'He's so not your parents' type either.'

'Would I see that as a problem?'

'OK, no. So now you tell me – what else?'

'How about – he already has a girlfriend?'

I groaned. 'Jeez, Arizona. Who is she?'

'Her name is Sable. She doesn't live in Ellerton.'

'Wait. Let me fill in the rest for myself. Sable is Kyle's girl – they're childhood sweethearts. He cheats on her and swears you to secrecy. But why would you agree?'

'I didn't know about Sable until after Kyle and I were an item. By that time I was hooked.'

'I don't see it, Arizona. Sure, Kyle is easy on the eye, but what else?'

'You mean, what did we talk about? Oh come on, Darina, when did talking become so necessary?'

'You may find this weird, but actually talking is cool.' I was thinking of me and Phoenix, naturally. And I wasn't liking the way Arizona had started talking down to me again. 'You should try it some time.'

'OK, you're right. And when I met Kyle at a party in Centennial I was at a point when I really needed someone to lean on. And I don't mean just physically. We danced and we talked – yes actually, he does do words of more than two syllables.'

126

'Did you tell Kyle about Raven?' I asked the litmus question. If yes, then it had been true love.

'Eventually I told him – we'd been together two months and I was feeling totally safe with him. That was when he opened up too and told me about Sable.'

'Thanks for that, Kyle!' I took on the sarcastic role for a change. 'Arizona, you needed that piece of information like a hole in the head.'

'Sable Jackson, the girl from Forest Lake.' Arizona closed her eyes at the memory. 'It turns out she and Kyle were engaged.'

'Oh God, Arizona!'

'I know – stupid, huh? I should've walked away. But it gets worse.'

'How worse? Isn't this as bad as it gets?'

'Fast forward another couple of months. I'm still into Kyle in every way. In spite of Sable, I escape from the house and spend every waking moment with him. I hang around after school outside Mike Hamill's place, waiting for Kyle to get out of work. One day we drive out to Amos Peak to be alone. It's our favourite place, and that's where I put pressure on him, give him an ultimatum and he tells me he can't give Sable up – not ever.'

'Does he tell you why not?' I'm hating Kyle Keppler more every second.

'She's pregnant,' Arizona said with the longest sigh. 'It's going to be a Christmas baby. They set their wedding for the last week in October.'

'So now that baby is nine months old, maybe ten.' Suddenly I was out of my league and looking to Phoenix for advice. Arizona and I had come down from the ridge and Lee had taken Arizona into the house to talk again with Hunter. Phoenix had been given the order to see me safely home.

'Living where?' he asked as we reached my car.

'Out of town, in Forest Lake. I guess Kyle Keppler went ahead and married Sable around the time Arizona died.'

'And Arizona hid this stuff because she didn't want his name dragged in. How does that follow?' Phoenix was assessing what I'd just told him, turning it around in his head. 'What was she doing – protecting him?'

I nodded, suddenly struck by something. 'The way she protected Raven all those years. That's what Arizona does when she loves someone – she builds a ring of silence around them.'

'But this puts Kyle in the right place – Mike's Motors, at the right time – the afternoon Arizona drowned. Plus, he has a motive.'

'For killing her?' I popped my lips then breathed out

sharply. 'Is that what we're looking at?'

'If it's not suicide, then it's murder.'

'Or an accident?' But then I remembered how Arizona had revisited the scene and felt someone was there, out at Hartmann, and how she'd felt a wave of fear. 'It sure feels like murder,' I agreed.

Phoenix hung his head, deep in thought. 'And this guy, Kyle – he sounds mean enough?'

'He hangs out with your brother, rides a Harley Dyna, stands around six feet four. That's all I know.'

'So don't go near him,' he begged, grabbing my hand. His voice grew urgent and intense. 'You hear me? Do what you have to do to help Arizona, but stay away from Kyle Keppler.'

6

The next day, Sunday, I was grounded.

Jim and Laura sat me down at the kitchen table and laid out the new boundaries. It went like this:

Jim: Your mother and I have been talking. We want to straighten out a few things.

Me: Go ahead – straighten.

Jim: We need an agreement from you that you won't leave the house at night.

Me: When you say 'night', what exactly are we saying? Would that be post-midnight, or post-10.00 p.m.? 8.00 p.m.? Earlier maybe?

Laura: Cut it out, Darina. Listen to what Jim has to say.

Jim: This is a dangerous town. Look at what happened to Summer. We . . . your mom is crazy with worry. She needs to know where you are – at school, at a friend's house, here in your room.

Me: That would be a twenty-four-seven curfew then?

Jim (grinding his teeth): We also need you to show more respect.

As soon as he introduced the 'R' word, he lost me. I went off into wondering where Phoenix was and what Arizona was doing right now. I remembered the last flash of Beautiful Dead action I'd been involved with the night before.

It was Lee Stone who had broken up Phoenix's 'Keep away from Kyle Keppler' speech. He'd run up the hill to tell Phoenix that Hunter needed him right now, that there was a bunch of weekenders at the Government Bridge camping ground who had drunk too much alcohol and were planning a late night ghost-busting trip up to Foxton Ridge.

'Do you have any names?' I'd asked, thinking maybe they would include Charlie Fortune and some other Ellerton vigilantes who every now and then decided to big themselves up by coming out to Foxton to nail widespread rumours of ghosts and weird happenings.

'Sorry, I don't.' Anyway, Lee pointed out he was new around there and names wouldn't mean much to him. 'Hunter said they're not from Ellerton.'

'Wow, your fame is spreading,' I'd muttered as Phoenix

kissed me goodbye. 'Soon the whole county will come looking.'

I'd sounded flippant, but I was seriously worried. The number of vigilantes who believed something weird was happening out at Foxton was growing. There was talk in the bars of figures seen on the ridge late at night, then came the story about the county surveyor who had been scared half crazy, and now the weird wind that had spooked Jenna Hall's horse. I wondered how long Hunter and the Beautiful Dead could keep the secret of their existence safe . . .

'Darina?' Laura brought me back with a jolt. 'You hear me? We're grounding you for the whole of today.'

Parents do that – they gang up against you by using the big 'we' all the time, like they're a huge army defending an empire and you're one small foot soldier.

'We want you to clean your room and then start on the kitchen. We want you to eat Sunday lunch with us then do all your schoolwork before supper. Did you hear what we said? You're not to leave the house.'

How many years was it since Laura had laid this one on me? What made her think it would work now?

Still, I decided not to put my head up above the stockade to get shot at – just for today I would stay grounded because I needed thinking and planning space.

132

I whizzed the vacuum cleaner over my rug. *Do I take Phoenix's parting advice and go to Brandon for more help?* I wondered.

'If things turn ugly, go find my brother,' he'd said as he ran down the hill with Lee.

Emptying my trash bucket into a black bag, I decided no. *Brandon shares information with Kyle Keppler*, I recalled, and no way did I want that to escalate. I'd agreed with Phoenix that I'd stay away from Kyle, so did I go out to Forest Lake and track down Sable instead? Taking out the trash, I decided yes, because we were running seriously short of time since Hunter's punishment. Yes, for sure – then tried to work out how I would find her address.

So maybe I would drive out to Forest Lake on the off chance, buy a cup of coffee in a diner, ask a few harmless questions . . .

'Hey, Darina, how did Miss Jones react?' Jordan cornered me after school next day. 'Did she rip you to pieces for dropping out of the concert so late into rehearsals?'

I was looking for a quick exit, wanting to head out to Forest Lake to follow my plan. 'She laid the guilt thing on me,' I muttered. 'But I don't care. I wanted out.'

'I don't blame you. I know how hard it is for you – since Phoenix.'

'Thanks.' *Don't be nice to me, Jordan!* Sympathy gets to me and makes me crumble.

'No way do I agree with Hannah,' she went on.

That's better – give me a sly, manipulative comment to grab hold of. 'Why – what does Hannah think? That I'm a wuss for dropping out, that I only ever think of myself and anyway I owe it to Summer, blah-blah?'

'All of the above,' Jordan nodded.

As it happened, Hannah was walking out of school with Logan. They were arm in arm, real cosy. I raised an eyebrow in their direction. 'Since when?' I asked Jordan.

'Why – do you care?' she smirked.

'No way!' The saying about protesting too much sprang to mind. My 'No way' had at least ten exclamation marks after it.

'Huh,' Jordan said, splitting off and leaving me free to head for my car.

I took another glance at Hannah and Logan. She had her mouth to his ear, whispering something. He shot a look in my direction then laughed. I got in my car.

Forest Lake was an hour out of Ellerton – a town that lived on its past, with an actual narrow-gauge steam railway, a museum and a row of shops selling hand-crafted saddles and Stetsons. Not many tourists make it this far though. The main street was deserted that Monday afternoon. I parked my car, walked past a shop selling Native American jewellery and greetings cards, into the only diner in town, where I ordered coffee and sat by a window overlooking the quiet street. Now that I was there, coming seemed like a dumb idea. With nothing better to do, I texted Laura to say I was at Jordan's house, doing schoolwork.

An old guy came in and ordered fresh doughnuts to go. A skinny white-and-brown dog walked along the sidewalk. Once in a while, a car drove into the parking lot of the convenience store opposite.

'Do you need anything to go with your coffee?' the waitress asked from behind the counter.

'No – thanks. Actually, I'm looking for Sable Jackson but I didn't bring her address with me.'

'Sorry, I can't help. I don't know any Sable Jackson.' The waitress wiped the top of the counter. 'We do have a Sable here in town, but she's Sable Keppler.'

'Sure.' I kicked myself for the mistake and tried to cover up with an embarrassed laugh. 'She married Kyle last year. I came over from Ellerton. I guess I'll drive on back and pick up her address.'

'No need.' More wiping – this time of the silver espresso machine. 'You'll find Sable's house right behind the main street, number 505 – turn left at the lights.'

I was up and out of there, my coffee undrunk. 'Thanks!' I called over my shoulder. I jumped in the car and drove to the lights, throwing a left as the waitress had told me. I crawled along a street called White Eagle Road, looking out for 505.

I wasn't expecting much, but Sable and Kyle's house didn't even meet the image I had in my mind. The house stood behind a wire fence that kept in two German shepherd dogs standing guard over a run-down shack with a broken porch. There was a child's stroller tipped on its side, grass growing up between the cracks in the yard. When I saw a woman talking to a man through the open door, I cruised on by.

So, from the glimpse I had, the woman was in her early twenties with straight black hair down to her waist, dressed in jeans and a white shirt – a smaller, less upmarket version of Arizona, I realized. The guy was also dark-haired . . . and definitely not Kyle Keppler.

At the top of the street, I turned the car and drove back down.

Sable and the guy were out on the porch now and the dogs were sniffing at the wheels of the Harley Softtail parked by the door. He put an arm around her waist to kiss her goodbye.

So Kyle cheated on her and now she's cheating on him. It was an obvious conclusion. *Where does the baby fit in? What happens when Kyle finds out?*

The guy stepped down from the porch, set the stroller upright, then started the Harley. He yelled something to Sable above the roar of the engine.

I was too busy quietly spying to hear or see a truck turn off the main street and pull up outside 505. It was only when the door slammed that I switched my attention to the driver and saw that it was Kyle.

Whoa! Suddenly I was in the middle of a Jerry Springer situation – 'My wife found out I'd cheated and is seeking revenge by openly sleeping around!'

I slowed to a stop and waited for the anger explosion.

Whoa again! Kyle picked his oil-stained denim jacket out of the back of the truck, unhitched a length of wire fence and stepped into the yard. The dogs bounded up to him. He said hi to the Harley guy and stopped to talk. Then he turned and spotted my bright-red convertible with me inside. It took him a while to compute – enough time for me to freeze and feel very afraid – then he got it: I was the nuisance kid who'd paid a visit to Mike's Motors to quiz him about Arizona.

Kyle Keppler moved fast for a big guy. The dogs barked as he sprinted out of the yard, across the street. I stepped on the gas just as he reached my car and grabbed the door handle. For a split second he dug in his heels and hung on as my tyres squealed from a standing start, then he let go.

In my mirror I saw the dark guy run to join him. The dogs were still barking and Sable was retreating into the house. I got out of Forest Lake and drove back to Ellerton, breaking every traffic regulation in the book.

I was still shaking when I reached home and found that Laura and Jim were out at work. I had the house to myself and plenty of time to regret what I'd just done. I took deep breaths, paced from room to room, tried to tell myself that Kyle hadn't recognized me after all.

'Darina?' Logan said, stepping on to the porch and peering in through the open kitchen window.

I jumped a mile. 'Don't creep up on me like that!' I yelled.

'I didn't creep – I knocked on the door. You didn't answer.'

'Maybe I chose not to,' I pointed out. 'What do you want, Logan?'

'I came to apologize. I know it looked like I was laughing at you, but I wasn't.'

'When? What are you talking about?'

'Earlier, with Hannah. I worked it through afterwards. It wasn't what you thought.'

'So you know what I'm thinking again?' I sighed, but inside I was glad for once for Logan's visit. 'Come in, tell me about it.'

He stooped as he came through the door, suddenly seeming taller than I'd realized and too big for our wooden kitchen chairs. 'Maybe Hannah – she might want it to be the way you saw it, her and me, you know – but it's so not true.'

'Did what you just said actually make sense?' I queried, deliberately making him suffer. 'Or is this some kind of riddle?'

'Hannah and I are not an item,' he announced after he'd drawn a deep breath. 'She asked me to go to the movies tonight but I turned her down.'

'And you needed to tell me?' My eyes were wide, I was still toying with him. 'Listen, Logan, feel free to go to the movies with Hannah any time you like.'

He frowned, leaned back on the flimsy chair, looked up at the ceiling. 'I hate what's happened between us lately,' he told me. 'When did we get into these games?'

It was my turn to take a breath. The way he looked at me, with hurt in his eyes, got through to me. 'When I fell in love with Phoenix?' I suggested. 'I'm serious. Ever since then, things went wrong for you.'

Slowly Logan let the front chair legs touch the ground. He nodded. 'You're right, it's true.'

'I can't help you. It happened. I loved – *love* Phoenix more than the world. You have to let me go.' I leaned across the table and touched his hand. 'Let me go, Logan, and we can be friends again.'

I thought maybe we took one small step in that direction before Laura came home from work and Logan left.

'Logan looked sad,' Laura remarked. She wore the jaded look she always had after a day selling cut-price clothes in the mall.

'We're *all* sad,' I told her, and that was enough to shut her up.

Next morning, early, Jim picked up a call on his way out of the house. 'Darina!' he yelled up the stairs. 'It's that old guy with the flowers – Peter Hall.'

I ran down two at a time to grab the phone. 'Peter, this is me. How's Jenna doing?'

'Jenna's good. It's Raven I'm calling about.'

'What happened to him? Where is he?'

'That's the problem. I just arrived at the house and you wouldn't believe the atmosphere. Frank was here, and

Allyson too. They told me they got a call from Raven's school. The kid's gone missing.'

'When?' I gasped.

'Early this morning. Possibly even late last night. Allyson's still on the phone, grilling them about when he was last seen. Frank already set off for the school in his car.'

'That's bad,' I groaned.

'Very bad.' Peter sounded cut up, his breathing was all wrong. 'I needed to talk. You're the only person I can tell.'

'So you need me to look out for Raven if he heads back to Ellerton?' It was hard to imagine that the kid would be able to make it alone, but I promised Peter anyway. 'What about you – what will you do? OK, don't answer that. Stay where you are. I'll come right over – we'll talk.'

Peter Hall met me at the Taylors' gate and quickly took me into an annexe to the side of the main house. 'We don't need to let anyone know you're here,' he explained.

'Any news?' I asked, taking in the orderly array of gardening tools, plant pots and fertilizers. There were magazines stacked neatly on a shelf and a corner of the room with a sink, a kettle and coffee mugs. 'Did they find Raven?'

Peter shook his head and tried hard to keep his voice

steady as he spoke. 'They decided he took off late last night – Frank just reached the school and called home. Allyson is speaking with the police department in Shepherd County.'

'Will she go and join Frank?'

'I doubt it. She's the type to leave the authorities to do their work while she continues on with her routine. Allyson knows Frank can deal with things at the school.'

'That's so not the point. How come she isn't going crazy like any other mother?'

'Allyson isn't any other mother,' he reminded me. 'Besides, this isn't the first time Raven has done this. The other times it worked out – either the school or the cops found him within a couple of hours and brought him back.'

'But this time you're not so sure?'

There was a pause. 'He never took off in the middle of the night before. Since Arizona passed, the stuff he's doing gets weirder.'

'He misses her,' I said quietly. 'Maybe he doesn't understand that she won't come back.'

Peter had his back to me and was staring out of the window, watching the main house. He stiffened as he saw the door open and Allyson Taylor walked out. 'Stay out of sight,' he warned.

I ducked back into a dark corner, hearing the sound of a car engine start up and the smooth swish of tyres down the drive.

'She's heading for the TV station,' Peter reported. 'It's OK, you can relax.'

'So did Raven run away before – when Arizona was around?' I wanted to know.

'A hundred times. Arizona and her parents fought over it all the time. She said it was obvious he wasn't happy at the school, they should bring him home. Frank and Allyson wouldn't listen.'

'And whose side were you on?'

He spread his hands, palms up. 'I'm no expert on autism. Not like Arizona – she read all the books, looked up every site on the internet. She even joined an organization dedicated to beating the condition through alternative treatments. She was sure she could help make Raven better. And the boy related to her and only her – his face would light up every time he saw her.'

'Yeah, that sounds like Arizona. She wouldn't sit back and do nothing.'

Peter badly needed to offload, so he spoke over me. 'She hated the medication they give him at the school. She'd read a theory that every kid with autism needs a shadow – someone to be a bridge between him and the outside world, to be at their side twenty-four seven to help them make sense of things.'

'Don't we all?' It sounded flip, but I meant it. 'Anyway, like I said – Arizona never did things by halves.'

'She would have done that for him – been his shadow,' he said, choking up. 'She would have given her life to help him.'

For the first time Peter paused, but I was falling apart now and didn't find any words to fill the gap.

'Like, on the day she died. It was a Thursday. Allyson and Frank were busy with work commitments, Raven was in school. Then the principal called home to tell Arizona he'd run away again.'

'What did she do?'

'She went crazy, accusing her dad, saying he should take Raven out of the school permanently even if Allyson disagreed.'

'And where did Raven go?' I wanted to know.

'He went looking for his sister, I guess. She ended up in the bottom of Hartmann Lake so he never found her.'

Poor kid – it must have been brutal. 'Arizona took her car for repair.' It was an unguarded moment and I spoke my next thought out loud. Any second Hunter's wings would be beating down a storm.

'Actually, yes. How did you know that?'

'Someone told me – I don't remember. Where did they eventually find Raven?'

'In town, wandering in the mall when the stores were closing.'

'And no one knew where he'd been all day?'

Peter took a deep breath. 'By that time, news was coming through about a body in Hartmann. We were too swallowed up by subsequent events to wonder where Raven had been hiding out.'

'I hear you,' I agreed. My mind was in overdrive – since Raven had gone looking for Arizona that awful day, was there any chance he'd found her? And if he had, did it make an impact on what had happened?

There were new questions and no one around to answer them – not Raven, for sure. Maybe Arizona though. I needed to get out to Foxton fast. 'I have to leave,' I told Peter. 'I skipped class to come here . . .'

'OK, you go,' he told me. 'But look out for Raven, will you? And don't tell anyone. I'm in trouble if Frank and Allyson find out I talked out of turn.'

'Sure. And you'll call me if – *when* they find him?' Hurriedly I gave him my cell number. 'Try not to worry, Peter. Raven always turns up – you said so yourself.'

'Maybe not this time,' he sighed. 'This time it feels different.'

'How, different?'

'Weird, as in spooky. It's like there's someone else, something else involved. I keep thinking of those rumours that are going around town, about ghosts or spirits walking the ridge out at Foxton. I'm not a guy who freaks out easily, don't get me wrong. But this time, just maybe—'

'Don't. You're giving me the creeps.' I faked a shudder as I left the annexe and hurried down the drive. I was thinking: *Arizona wouldn't . . . even she wouldn't use her zombie powers to spirit her beloved kid brother out of his school . . .*

I was driving over the limit again and I'd reached the cross out at Turkey Shoot when Phoenix and Arizona materialized right beside me inside the car. They appeared in their fuzzy-edged halos of light, shimmering into their solid shapes as shock made me swing out towards the central reservation.

'Pull over,' Phoenix said, no greetings, no loving smile. 'We were at Westra, at Arizona's house. We heard everything Peter told you.'

I turned the wheel and crunched on to the dirt-covered hard shoulder, raising dust and insects into the still, warm air.

From the back seat, Arizona answered the biggest of my panicky, unspoken questions. 'I had nothing to do with this, Darina. Raven made his own decision to take off, just like always.'

'You didn't take him out of school?' I asked, turning in my seat to see the new, real Arizona – no more Miss Cool, but instead a crazy-eyed girl with hair flopping over her face whose kid brother was missing.

'Why would I?' she demanded.

'Because you hate the place, you wanted your parents to take him away.'

She stared at me, reading deep into my thoughts. 'That was back then,' she said quietly. 'When he had me to come home to.'

'I get it,' I nodded. 'Sorry.'

'Come on, Darina,' Phoenix cut in. 'We're going to join the search for Raven. You'll be our link to the far side, like always.'

'Where do we start?' Again I turned to Arizona, this time for guidance. 'Where does he head when he runs away?'

Phoenix answered for her. 'He usually doesn't get far, so we're going to start on the school premises. There'll be cops – we have to take care.'

'Which way?'

'Back towards town.' Arizona spoke with a hint of robot – too calm, too distant – to mask her panic. 'Turn west before we get there, along the Peak Road.'

I turned the car around, thinking through the directions and ending up with a chill running down my spine. 'That road leads to Hartmann.'

'Yeah.'

'So?'

'So it also leads to the Lindsey Institute, fifteen minutes down the road at the foot of Amos Peak. On a good day Raven can see the lake from his bedroom window.'

So I drove my two Beautiful Dead passengers down to Hartmann Lake, feeling the restless tension build. Phoenix sat beside me, his dark hair lifting in the wind, staring ahead and hyper-aware, as if every tree or rock we passed held information about the missing kid. In the back seat, Arizona sank down as we passed Hartmann, unable to look at the place where she'd drowned.

'You remember – Raven pulled this same stunt the day "it" happened?' I queried, trying to focus on the road ahead, though the glittering water distracted me and the horror of what had taken place there. 'Peter reckons Raven came looking for you.'

'I hear you.' Arizona's non-committal reply was almost too quiet to notice.

'He didn't find you?' I checked her expression in my overhead mirror.

She closed her eyes, her lips barely moved. 'After I was through shouting at my dad, I went to Mike's Motors. Raven wouldn't know to look for me there. As far as I can recall, we didn't hook up.'

I glanced at Phoenix to check that this time Arizona was telling me the truth. He gave a slight nod. 'Tell me something, Mister Zombie – how come everything turns into a blur around the "event"?' It had been the same with Jonas – when he came back to the far side, courtesy of his overlord, the all-powerful Hunter, his memory of the actual crash was wiped. 'You and Summer – you don't remember either.'

'Not the details,' he admitted. 'Hunter says it's the trauma of the occasion that does it – it kind of scrambles your brain. You have a tiny amount of recall – maybe a smell or a colour around what happened – but the thing itself is wiped. That's why we're here, to bring it back, set it straight and get free.'

'Until then we're trapped.' Arizona's tone was bitter. 'Here in this nowhere place – dead but not at peace, here but not here, not able to trust anyone or to take a moment's rest. You have no idea, Darina, of what that feels like.'

The wind hit the windshield then caught us in a swirling gust. I blinked hard. *Keep the car on the road!* I told myself. Straight ahead was Amos Peak, blue-grey in the distance, already snow-capped in late October.

'You're right – I have no idea,' I agreed. 'But like you, Arizona, the deeper I get into this, the less I can trust people, I tell you that for sure.'

Raven's school, a low-rise development of log-cabin units built around a small manmade lake, was called the Lindsey Institute after the guy who founded it in the nineteen-sixties. When we reached there, at about twelve noon, instead of a place crawling with cops we found a single sheriff's car by the main door to a big, ranch style building, with Frank Taylor's red Mitsubishi parked alongside.

'They're sure putting everything they've got into this search,' Arizona said bitterly. I'd parked outside the gates from where we could look down on the school.

'Hey, at least it makes it easier for Darina to snoop around,' Phoenix reminded her. 'I guess the log cabins are where the kids sleep, but what about the main building?'

'That's where they have lessons, therapy, visits from family.' This was getting harder for Arizona as the painful memories flowed. 'Everything looks low tech and friendly, but this place is a prison camp, believe me.'

'So where do I start?' I got out of the car and looked for a back entrance I could reach on foot, spotting a narrow track across some scrub ground that I planned to take. 'What happens if I bump into someone – what's my excuse?'

'You're smart, Darina, you decide,' she said sharply, then sighed. 'Sorry, forget I said that. The staff here don't look like medics, they dress in jeans and sneakers, even the principal, Rebecca Davis. She's slim built with curly blonde hair, but don't let appearances fool you. If you run into her, watch out.'

'She'll be with Frank and the sheriff,' Phoenix suggested. 'Skirt around the back of the main building to start with. If someone asks, say you're a tourist. You lost your way coming away from Hartmann.'

'Raven usually stays close to the school when he does this,' Arizona explained. 'He knows he needs to leave but he doesn't have any idea where he wants to go, so he walks up into the pine trees or goes to sit by the lake. Or maybe he'll wander along the creek and gets as far as the Pooles' place a mile downstream. That's the furthest he ever got.'

'We'll try the creek,' Phoenix decided. 'Darina, you search closer to the buildings.'

'I'd put my money on you two any time,' I grinned. 'Given that you hear every leaf fall.' I set off down the hill not too worried but anxious to stay out of Frank Taylor and Rebecca Davis's way. My excuses would have to be more sophisticated if I bumped into them.

I'd covered half the distance when the front door opened and a blonde woman walked out with a guy in uniform – the local sheriff. I dropped back behind a convenient rock, waiting for them to finish their conversation. While I was there, I studied a parking lot at the back of the building where the staff most likely left their cars and deliveries were made. I watched a kitchen guy exit the building and throw a bag in the trash container. Then he stood, arms folded, staring up at the sky.

Go back inside! I willed him. *I'm stymied with you standing there.*

Eventually the kitchen worker left off gazing and went back to work. I edged down the hill until I was a hundred metres from the parking lot, then I had another scare as the sheriff got into his patrol car and set off up the track, only to stop halfway up the hill and step out. Then I was down behind another rock, holding my breath and waiting again.

The sheriff spoke into his two-way radio, leaning

against the side of his car, taking his time. 'Wes, do you copy? Yeah, it's the usual kid – Raven Taylor.' His voice was faint but I could just make it out. 'Staff reported him missing at breakfast this morning. Over.' There was a pause while he listened, then he spoke again. 'The father is here. Rebecca has staff out searching the grounds. So far, they didn't find him. Over.'

Leaving the sheriff to report back to base and decide on his next move, I carried on down the hill, creeping towards the giant trash can that would give me good cover, all the time not really believing that it would be me who found the missing boy. I was crouching low and working my way between a black Jeep and a silver SUV when I heard the first noise.

It came from the SUV – a faint tapping sound which stopped then started again, as if somebody inside the car was knocking a small object against a metal surface. I caught my breath. What did I do now? If I suddenly popped up in view, what would the person in the car think? If I carried on with my stealth assault, the game was up anyway. The tapping happened again and I stood up.

At first I thought I'd made a mistake – there was no one inside the car after all. Then I looked and listened again. Tap-tap-tap from the back of the vehicle – the section behind a metal grille meant for bags or dogs. I went round to the rear window and took another good look inside.

The kid was sitting cross-legged in the baggage space, a book resting across his knees, a sketch pad by his side. He was rocking back and forth, locked in his world, tapping his metal pen against the grille.

Without thinking, I opened the door. Raven didn't stop rocking or tapping. The book in his lap showed a picture of the famous Warhol Marilyns, all sunshine yellows and oranges, purple hair and crimson, pouting lips.

'Hi, Raven,' I whispered.

He rocked and tapped as if I wasn't there.

'What are you doing here?'

He ran the pen along the mesh grille, like a pianist running a finger along the keys. The cover of the pad by his side was covered in tiny, complex sketches of his house in Westra.

'Hey, I like your drawings,' I told him, and he looked up at me. I offered him my hand. He took it.

Of course, Phoenix and Arizona knew the second I found Raven. They were there by my side in an instant, in the parking lot to keep an eye on me but staying out of sight as I gently helped the kid from the vehicle.

'And I really love these,' I told him as he let me take the

Marilyn pictures away from him. 'Pick up your sketch book, let's go get some lunch.'

He frowned then stiffened, turning back towards the SUV. Every movement was slow and a little clumsy. The way he moved, he reminded me of one of those old-fashioned puppets on strings.

'You want to stay here? That's cool.' *Why this car?* I wondered, then the answer came to me in a flash – that Arizona had the exact same car as this! *Same model, same colour.* 'I like this car. It's cool.'

Poor kid – the only place in the world he felt safe was in that stranger's vehicle, believing that his sister would soon come to fetch him.

Out of the corner of my eye I saw Phoenix take Arizona's hand and hold it tight.

'If you don't want lunch, how about coming to see your dad?' I tried a different tack. 'He's here on a visit.'

There was no response – no reluctance, no eagerness, just a big blank.

Arizona took a step forward but Phoenix held her back. I knew that if she showed herself, they would have to take Raven and zap his already damaged brain clean of the memory.

Boy, was she having the hardest time as she agreed to step back. Think about it – all she wanted to do was the one thing she couldn't, which was to throw her arms around her brother, hug him and tell him everything would be OK.

'Arizona, you need to leave,' Phoenix told her.

She raised her hand to cover her eyes, clutching at her temples and holding back the sobs.

'You have to go before you tear yourself apart,' he insisted. 'I'll take care of things here.'

She took a half a step towards her brother then faltered.

'Come and see your dad,' I insisted, tapping the cover of the Marilyn book as a kind of bait. 'Come with me.'

'Go!' Phoenix whispered to Arizona.

Finally she gave in. I walked around the side of the ranch house with Raven just as she used her power to disappear. There was the bright halo of light, quickly fading and then an absence. Phoenix stood alone.

'Take him in the house. Make sure you hand him over to Rebecca Davis.' Phoenix was the calmest, the strongest of Raven's team of would-be rescuers.

'So tell me about your favourite picture,' I said to the kid, trying to keep the shakes out of my voice. 'Would it be these Marilyns or the cool soup cans that you like the most?'

7

'Did you see Frank Taylor?' Phoenix wanted to know. He was at the wheel of my car, driving us back towards Hartmann Lake. I'd handed Raven over to the principal, made a lame excuse and left.

'I found the kid in the forest,' I'd told her. 'I figured he belonged here.'

You should have seen the way Raven looked at me when Rebecca Davis took control – hurt and confused doesn't really hit the mark, but it's the best I can do. He thought we two were yellow and red, purple and green Marilyn buddies and now here I was, dumping him back with the grey people.

'So, did you?' Phoenix repeated.

'Uh, no – luckily, Frank wasn't around.' I had to stop feeling sorry for Raven and focus on our next step. 'I got out of there as fast as I could, before Rebecca could ask me any awkward questions.'

'Cool.' Phoenix drove for a while.

'How is it, being Raven – not talking, not getting other people, just living inside a bubble?' I wondered. 'Pretty lonely, I guess. And think, Phoenix – if the kid was able to talk, all the answers he could give us. Like where he went the morning Arizona drowned, who he saw, how come he ended up in the mall . . .'

He glanced my way then back at the road ahead. 'You want to know something weird?' he murmured. 'Back there in the parking lot I tried to read Raven's thoughts, but I couldn't do it.'

'That's crazy!' Phoenix and the Beautiful Dead had amazing telepathic powers. 'What happened?'

'I tried and there was nothing – just a jumble of stuff.'

'Maybe you didn't have enough time.' I offered excuses. 'And Arizona was finding it tough. There was a lot going on.'

'No.' Phoenix stopped me. 'The fact is – the kid's brain is wired up differently. No way could I get through to him.'

We were both silent then, driving by Hartmann. The fall sun glittered gold on the clear green water. On the far bank a lone deer drank.

'I have some news about the latest bunch of vigilantes.' Phoenix restarted the conversation as we pulled on to metalled road and headed for town. 'You know the guys who came looking for trouble at the weekend?'

'The ones who camped out at Government Bridge?'

'Yeah. Well, Kyle Keppler was there, and his buddies from Forest Lake.'

The news made me groan. 'That guy's like a bad smell – real hard to shake off. You know I went over there yesterday?'

Phoenix nodded. 'Even though I said to stay away.'

'I didn't reckon on him being there.'

'You shouldn't go near him or his place, Darina.'

'Aren't you listening to me? I figured he'd be working at Mike's. I needed to talk with Sable. Did she find out about Kyle and Arizona? If she did, what exactly did she do about it?'

'Too risky,' he insisted then clenched his teeth as he took a bend a shade too fast, throwing me against him.

I pulled myself upright and clamped my mouth tight shut. Another period of silence followed.

'OK, so I'm doing it all wrong!' I burst out at last. 'Arizona said way back that I was too dumb to help you guys. Now you believe it too!'

'I didn't say that,' he sighed then he pulled the car

159

down a dirt track to the side of the road. We stopped beside a field of yellow grass with a barn in the distance. 'You know I worry about you, Darina.'

'No need,' I protested. But I didn't fool him. 'OK, so you worry about me. Thank you.' I smiled and kissed him.

He gave a sad little sigh. 'All this is happening to you because of me – all the pain and doubt. I wish it didn't have to be like this.'

'I wouldn't have it any other way.' I needed Phoenix to know this. 'Every second we spend together is a gift. I don't care what it costs.'

He gazed at me, the long golden grass sloping up towards the mountains behind his head, his eyes shining beautiful and blue. 'Stay safe for me,' he whispered, then he kissed me softly on the lips. 'And let me worry – OK?'

'OK,' I smiled.

'And this has nothing to do with you being dumb.'

'For sure?' I asked, gazing into those eyes.

'Trust me,' he murmured, kissing me again to make certain I believed him. 'Darina, I love you.'

'But?'

'No buts.'

'So we didn't just have another fight?' I leaned in and

kissed him back. I had that achingly awesome feeling of being closer to Phoenix than any two people had ever been or ever could be.

'Take it easy,' he told me, climbing out of the car and waiting for me to reverse back on to the highway.

'I love you!' I mouthed.

'I love you,' he replied.

My heart soared.

For the longest time I kept him in sight in my rearview mirror – standing there with his feet wide apart and his thumbs hooked into his belt, watching me go.

Minutes later I was wishing I still had Phoenix in the car with me.

The incident started with a truck coming fast from behind and overtaking me on a bend.

'Dumb driver!' I slammed on my brakes to let the truck get by. 'What's with you?'

Now the truck driver tucked in front of me and braked suddenly, his tail lights glowing red under the pinewood canopy.

I braked again, with some full-on cursing. That was until I recognized the guy hanging out of the passenger window as the Harley rider I'd seen in the Kepplers' yard – the one who'd been giving Sable the over-friendly hug. Then it felt like I'd been kicked in the stomach. I slowed to a halt, praying for the truck to disappear out of sight.

But no, the driver up ahead performed a spectacular U-turn in the narrow road. He headed back towards me, and I could see it was Kyle Keppler himself at the wheel, with his dark-haired buddy still hanging out of the passenger side, yelling wild insults. The truck stopped and I got ready for a face-off.

First Kyle and then his Neanderthal friend stepped down from the cab. They walked slowly towards me. The friend stopped maybe three metres from my car, while Kyle came right up.

'Honey, this is where your luck runs out,' he sneered. 'You get away from me one time, and one time only.'

'What did I do?' I protested, my heart thumping in my chest. More in hope than belief, I looked in my rearview mirror for Phoenix.

Kyle wasn't about to enter into explanations. His fist landed against my windscreen then he wrenched open my door and reached inside.

I struggled, but the guy was too strong. He lifted me out of there like I was a rag doll, then dumped me in the scrubland at the side of the road. I staggered back against the rough surface of a granite rock.

'Real cool car,' the buddy in the background said. He was carrying a steel bar that I hadn't seen until then. 'Yeah – it's a freaking shame.'

By now my heart had broken through my chest, it was pounding up in my throat, making me gag with fear. Kyle Keppler gave the other guy a signal and I heard the metal bar whack into the hood of my car.

'That could be your skull,' Keppler told me, pressing me hard against the boulder. 'Jeez, what a mess.'

I knew my legs wouldn't hold me up. I felt myself sinking to the ground. Then in a nanosecond everything changed.

Phoenix appeared in his halo of light, solid out of nowhere, taking a swing at Keppler, who saw him just in time and ducked. His buddy tossed him the steel bar and he caught it.

Some people scream in terror. I found I couldn't utter a sound.

Now Keppler wielded the bar like a baseball bat. He swung it at Phoenix's head.

'Where the crap did he come from?' the guy in the background yelled, crouching behind Phoenix like a football defender, trying to trap him against the banking.

The bar missed Phoenix's face by centimetres. Phoenix dived in to butt Keppler in the stomach and send him

163

staggering back towards me. 'Stand clear,' he warned.

Keppler raised the bar and smashed it down once, twice more. Each time he grunted as he missed, too slow to land a blow as Phoenix moved smoothly from side to side.

But it was two against one and I could see the other guy moving in, sticking out his foot to trip Phoenix and pin him to the ground while Keppler towered over him, ready with the bar.

I found my voice and yelled for Phoenix to watch out.

With one hand he stayed the bar in mid-air, with the other he shoved the accomplice so hard that the guy toppled and slid half under my car. Now with both hands free, Phoenix turned his full zombie strength on Keppler. He tore the bar from his hands and beat him back against the rocks. The bar was at Keppler's throat, forcing his head back and making his eyes roll in his skull. I filled my time stamping on guy number two's hands as he tried to crawl from under the car.

'Don't you ever touch Darina!' Phoenix was centimetres from Keppler's distorted features. 'You lay one finger on her and you're dead!'

Then he flung the bar away. It fell with a clatter as he landed a punch on Keppler's jaw, sending him sideways, grovelling in the dirt alongside his buddy.

'I ought to kill you for this,' Phoenix muttered.

'Don't!' I begged. *No more fights. No hidden blades, please!*

Our brief conversation had given the two guys a fraction of breathing space – long enough for them to be up on their feet and coming at Phoenix together.

This time I did scream.

Phoenix took hold of Keppler's swinging fist and sent him crashing against the dark-haired guy, flinging them both against my car, making it look so easy.

'OK, enough,' he decided out loud. 'This is going to hurt real bad.'

Then he stared into their eyes – the sidekick first, then Keppler – zapping them with the full force of his mind-blowing power.

A sudden, fierce wind kicked up and I saw the dirt rise, heard the wings begin to beat. Millions of wings – hordes of dead souls released from limbo who gave Phoenix his ability to wipe memories clean, leaving the victims empty and aching, waking up later and wondering what the hell happened and how they came to be lying in the dirt covered in bruises.

At first Keppler resisted. He tried to lunge again towards Phoenix, but my Beautiful Dead boyfriend stood his ground, his gaze fixed on him like a laser into his brain. Keppler staggered backwards, into his buddy, and they hit the ground together.

Countless wings raised the dust storm high into the blue sky as Phoenix stood proud and victorious.

'Brandon will take your car for repair,' Phoenix promised me.

We'd had to leave it in the ditch and walk into town before Keppler and his buddy came round.

I was dazed, my head refused to work clearly after the shock. 'Logan will do that. I only have to ask him and Christian – they'll work on the car together.'

'Brandon,' Phoenix insisted. 'Tell him where we left it. He'll tow it in.'

'Just tell him not to take it to Mike's Motors,' I joked. 'OK, not funny, huh? And before you say I told you so about Keppler, I admit it – you were right.'

'Brutal guy,' Phoenix confirmed.

We walked slowly along a rough sidewalk, with no one around. The lost souls had packed up their wings and gone wherever they called home. 'Tell me what you know about him, besides the Arizona connection.'

Phoenix stuck his hands deep into his jeans pockets before he dropped the bombshell. 'The guy with him – that was Sable's brother, Jon Jackson.'

'Her brother!' I hadn't thought of that when I ran my

Jerry Springer scenario, back in the Kepplers' front yard. I had him down as a love rival, remember. OK, so I have this personality defect of rushing headlong, and here's another example.

'Jon was at Government Bridge with Kyle and a couple of others. They like to hang out together.'

'Would Brandon be included in the gang?' I wanted to know exactly where Rohr Brother Senior fitted in. 'Brandon, Kyle and Jackson – they're a team?'

'Sometimes.' Phoenix clammed up, lowering his gaze and walking slightly ahead. 'Look – I don't choose my brother's buddies!'

I thought this through. 'OK, I get it. You don't want to drag Brandon in because Kyle's not a nice person to be around and you'd rather I didn't paint Brandon with the same brush. Is that right?'

A nod was all I got by way of reply.

I ran to catch him up. 'Plus, Kyle and Jackson – they were there on . . . on the night!' The fact hit me between the eyes – they'd been members of the killer gang that gathered by the petrol station in town. 'Phoenix, they were part of what happened to you!'

He shook his head.

'Does that mean yes or no?' I grabbed his hand and made him slow down. 'Look at me and tell me the truth.'

'They were there,' he admitted. 'Along with maybe twenty other guys. But we don't need to focus on that right now. This is about Arizona, remember.'

'Jeez, how could she even *like* this guy?' We were walking again, almost within sight of the first houses on the Peak Road into town.

'Arizona *loved* Kyle,' he reminded me. Liking and loving – they're not the same thing.'

'So what now?' I meant, what was our next move, once I'd been to Brandon and got him to take care of my crushed car hood. 'Do I make another move to get Sable alone and ready to talk?'

'No way.'

'We only have three days to do this, remember!' Friday was racing towards us, the final deadline set by Hunter. 'So do I confront the Taylors over Raven – push them to spill the guilty family secrets?'

'That works better,' he said. Our pace was slowing. We could see the houses and it was past time for Phoenix to leave.

'Maybe it goes like this. Arizona fights all the time with her parents – her mom especially. She wants Raven back home, is ready to give up everything to be with him twenty-four seven, to be the kind of shadow she believes he needs.'

Phoenix nodded. 'You mean, she *really* fights with Allyson. It turns nasty and the family is falling apart. Frank is too weak to stop it happening.'

My turn to nod. I'm talking faster. 'And you know Arizona – when she figures she's right she doesn't let go. Allyson too. They're two immoveable forces. In the end, it has to end violently.'

'Maybe,' Phoenix said, almost too quiet to hear.

'It's possible! Picture it. Just how unfeeling can we figure Allyson to be? Here's a mom who didn't stay home from work even when her autistic son ran away from school. You hear of unnatural mothers like her, you read it in the newspaper, you don't expect ever to see one. But maybe this is Monster Mom in the flesh!'

'So they finally fight out by Hartmann.' Phoenix picked up the last threads of my latest theory. 'Arizona is out there looking for Raven, Allyson tracks her there . . .'

'And accuses Arizona of knowing where the kid is, this is down to her, she's one crazy girl hiding her brother from the authorities . . .'

'They struggle by the water's edge. There's an accident – Arizona slips and falls in . . .'

I'm nodding like crazy. This really could be the key to unlock Arizona's mystery. With three days to go, we were almost there.

'But Arizona can swim.' Phoenix put on the brakes. 'She won medals at junior school.'

Now I was dead set on nailing Monster Mom. 'She hit her head as she fell, went unconscious, sank right to the bottom.' I stopped as the rough track turned to paved sidewalk. 'Don't come any further,' I warned.

'You want me to leave?' he asked with that lopsided half-grin.

'Hunter will know if you come any further. You have to go back to Foxton.' I pushed him away. He caught both my hands in his. 'Go!' I gasped.

We kissed for a long time before he drew back.

'You'll never guess,' he laughed, then broke off his sentence as if he was embarrassed.

'What? . . . Phoenix, there's a car coming!' I heard it higher up the street, growing louder.

'Hunter says I can stay.'

'Stay here with me? Not go back to Foxton?'

'We know Kyle Keppler will come after you again. Hunter says I have to be here to take care of you.'

I gasped, feeling my whole body glow. 'The whole day? Is that what you're saying?'

'And night,' he promised, putting his arm around my waist and drawing me behind some high advertising boards, out of sight of the passing car.

Phoenix was there in my room, sitting on the bed, waiting for me. We'd said goodbye on the outskirts of town and I'd walked on alone. He'd already checked in with Hunter and the Beautiful Dead out at Foxton and was still at my house before me.

'You need to see Brandon about your car,' Mister Sensible insisted.

'Tomorrow,' I argued. I didn't want any interruptions to our alone time.

'Now. They forecast rain. Call him – ask him to tow it in.'

Sighing, I took out my phone.

Brandon answered my call almost before the dialling tone kicked in. 'Darina, what's up?'

'My car is what's up.'

'Did you crash it?' He jumped to the obvious conclusion as if the idea amused him.

'No. It got smashed up. Your friend Kyle Keppler forced me off the road. His brother-in-law performed acts of violence with an iron bar.'

'Why would he do that?' The tone changed and Brandon's question came back sharp and suspicious.

I glanced at Phoenix, who had got up from the bed and was standing by the window. 'Kyle doesn't like me, that's all I can tell you.'

'That's a whole heap of dislike, for two guys to do that to your car. Were you hurt?'

'No, I'm cool. But my car isn't. I was hoping you could fix to have it towed in for repair.'

Brandon didn't hesitate. He checked that I was home and told me to wait. 'I'll pick you up. You can show me where the car is.'

Sighing, I came off the phone. 'So how do I explain this to your brother?' I asked Phoenix.

'Say it has to do with Arizona.' He suggested that a half-truth would be enough. 'Brandon knew about her and Kyle, remember.'

I nodded. 'OK, that'll work. He'll think Kyle got mad with me for meddling somehow in his personal life. And he'll know the guy has a temper.'

'Believe me, Brandon won't ask questions. He'll take care of you, like he told me he would.'

With his last breath Phoenix had made his brother promise to be my protector. Brandon had held him in his arms and sworn on his life.

'And I really have to go with him?' I sighed as I put my arms around Phoenix's neck. 'When all I want is to stay here with you.'

He smiled, and we worked on improving the physical

side of our relationship before the throaty roar of Brandon's Harley engine interrupted us.

'Go!' Phoenix said, unpeeling my arms. 'I'll be here when you get back.'

I rode pillion on Brandon's Dyna, using his broad back as a shield from the wind, feeling the flick of his fringed jacket against my arms. We drove towards the Peak Road under the storm clouds that Phoenix had warned about.

When we drew level with my car, he braked and pulled across the road. We both got off the bike and walked slowly around the car.

'Kyle and Jon did this?' Brandon checked with me. The metal bar had crumpled the hood pretty good. The windshield was smashed and one of the wing mirrors was hanging loose. 'Those guys were out of control.'

I nodded. 'It was scary.'

Brandon narrowed his eyes. 'OK, I don't need to know why.'

Trying to look helpless and innocent wasn't easy for me, so my don't-ask-me shrug wouldn't have won any Oscars.

'I'll handle this, Darina. You'll get your car back good as new.'

'And that was it,' I told Phoenix, taking off my wet denim jacket and hanging it over the chair by my desk. 'You were right – no questions, no lies.'

He was waiting by the window when Brandon dropped me off at the house, taking care to stay out of sight. By now, cold rain was falling and dusk came down before it was due.

So Phoenix's plan to enlist Brandon's help had worked. Brandon would tow the car to a garage, then pay a visit to Kyle's house. He and Kyle would come to an understanding for Kyle to stay away from me from now on.

'Thanks,' I told Phoenix as he handed me a towel for my dripping hair. More sounds outside the house told me that Laura was home from work. 'Wait here,' I whispered.

Downstairs, Laura was tired, so what was new? She kicked off her shoes and sat down with a beer. 'The wind's whipping up a storm,' she predicted. 'So where's your car, Darina? I didn't see it in the driveway.'

'The windshield wiper came loose.' (*True, actually.*) 'Brandon Rohr is going to fix it.' (*Also true.*)

'That's nice. Did you eat yet?'

'I had pizza.' (*Not true.*)

'You should eat better, Darina.' (*True.*)

'So where's Jim?'

'Out of state. He won't be home.'

'You don't need to fix a meal since I already ate.' I hovered by the foot of the stairs. 'I have to work on my science project.'

'So go,' Laura sighed, putting her feet up on the couch and resting her head against a cushion.

Phoenix lay beside me in my room. We listened to the raindrops against the window panes, we stared out at a black sky.

I was more alive than I ever remember, my heart bursting with joy.

We lay on our backs, our arms stretched above our heads, fingers intertwined, staring into each other's eyes. I curled in towards him, he didn't move, and we lay there for an age. Then he kissed my forehead. I raised my face up towards him and let his lips touch mine. More alive and aching, kissing him, being kissed.

The rain beat against the window.

I wanted this to last, knew that it couldn't. This was the way it would have been . . .

Before midnight the storm broke. It rolled in on a stronger wind that brought thunder and lightning that split the sky in two.

Phoenix sat up and swung his legs over the edge of the bed. He pressed a trembling hand against his forehead.

'What is it – the storm?' I was torn out of my paradise and suddenly afraid. An electric storm was the biggest danger the Beautiful Dead encountered here on the far side – it weakened them and robbed them of their powers, made them vulnerable to their enemies.

'I have a pain, here.' Phoenix took my hand and guided my fingers to the angel-wing tattoo below his shoulder blade.

'Is it bad?' I asked as I stroked his smooth, cold skin then leaned forward to kiss the wings once, twice, three times.

'You make it feel better,' he murmured. 'Darina . . .'

'I know . . . you have to leave,' I whispered quickly. 'The others are waiting for you on Foxton Ridge.'

He stood up and raised me with him, wrapped his arms around me and breathed the words against my cheek. 'I want to be with you, I swear!'

'I love you. Go.'

'In the morning, come out to the ridge. Wait for me there.'

Lightning forked across the sky, wind rattled the

window frame. Fear made me shake from head to toe. 'Go,' I begged. 'Leave, before it's too late.'

The storm raged all night long – rain and wind, a black sky shot through with jagged lightning strikes. I lay on my bed telling myself by tortured degrees that Phoenix would have made it back to Foxton, would have met up with Hunter and the Beautiful Dead and by now they would be long gone from the far side, somewhere safe on the other side of the grave. I would go up there in the morning, once the storm had cleared.

Thursday and Friday – that's all we have, I told myself. *So how am I going to get up to Foxton without my car?* I sat up in bed as thunder rolled overhead.

Now that I had no transport, it was as if my legs had been cut from under me.

Whoa, what do I do?

Maybe I set out now, in the middle of the storm. I hitch a ride out of Centennial, get dropped off at the Foxton junction, walk up to the ridge and be at the barn by dawn.

I was climbing into my jeans and shirt, pulling on my boots when Hunter appeared.

The room filled with silver light. He materialized by the window, the storm pounding against the panes. I thought my mind had flipped and I was totally crazy.

'You shouldn't be here!' I gasped, rooted to the spot. 'Where's Phoenix? Where are the others?'

'Safe,' he replied. In the shimmering light, I saw that he was shaking. Water ran from his hair, down his granite face. His eyes were so dark and sunken that for a moment I was scared he'd become one of the death-heads raised from limbo to terrify far-siders who strayed too close to the barn.

'You should be with them.' If he stayed any longer, he would be too wounded and weakened to leave. 'Why are you here?'

'I need you,' Hunter confessed. A flash of lightning tore the sky and made him shudder. He put one hand against my desk to steady himself.

This still didn't compute. Hunter was strong and firm – unshakeable. He shouldn't be weak and trembling. 'Need me – how?'

'Come with me,' he pleaded. 'Quickly.'

'Where?' I was ready to travel with him, if he still had the power. I got ready for the wings to start beating, for the light to surround me.

'To Foxton.'

'What for?' Here they came – the rush of wings, the strong gust of cold, wet air as Hunter opened the bedroom window.

'To find Lee Stone,' Hunter told me. He took my hand and, surrounded by the storm of strong wings, lifted me out of the house, into the night. 'Lee didn't make it,' he explained as the eerie force tore at my face, my hair, every muscle and bone in my body. 'He's still here on the far side. You have to come.'

When you travel with the overlord of the Beautiful Dead, you don't fly or float, spin or drift. It's like you're caught in the eye of a tornado, held there until you arrive in the place he wants you to be. Then you fall a million miles through blackness before you come around.

We were at the Foxton junction. It was still night-time and the storm was as bad as ever.

I had to hold on to Hunter to be able to stand up against the wind blowing down from the ridge. He was still shaking, his eyes more black and sunken. Rain trickled down his temple, over the faded angel-wing tattoo where he'd been shot through the head.

'Lee was down here when the weather broke,' Hunter whispered, his shoulders hunched and teeth chattering like a man freezing to death. 'The electric storm hurt him too bad – he couldn't get back.'

Gasping, I took a look around at the row of fishermen's shacks by the racing creek. All except one stood in darkness.

Hunter staggered through the wind and rain towards the single light. 'I came looking after I sent the others back. Don't worry, Darina – Phoenix is safe for sure.'

'But you're not!' I cried. I stumbled over my own feet it was so pitch black. 'Every second you stay here, you get weaker!'

'I'm here for Lee,' he said through gritted teeth. 'The guy staying in this shack – he found Lee where he'd fallen, down by the creek. He dragged him under cover before I could get to him. I guess he thought he was doing good.'

'Under cover – where?' Slowly I was getting my breath back, starting to think. It was clear I had to get Lee out of the rescuer-guy's hands and back in tow with Hunter. Then the two of them could get the hell out.

'He took him inside the house.'

'How long do I have?' I asked, calculating that I could hammer on the door and draw the man outside while Hunter stayed invisible and snuck in while the guy's back was turned.

'Not long.' Hunter could hardly open his mouth to speak, he was so weak. I saw that he was risking everything for Lee. 'The lightning got to him. He passed out. Go, Darina!'

I stumbled forward, up the step on to the porch. I used my fist to beat at the wooden door.

At first no one came. Inside the shack the guy was probably thinking that no way was he about to open his door to a second stranger on a night like this. Then maybe he thought someone had come looking for Lee, so the door gave a fraction.

I saw a pair of glittering eyes through the narrow slit. 'Help – you've got to come!' I yelled, my hair plastered to my skull, rainwater streaming from me. 'My car got stuck in the gulley out at the junction. I need you to tow me out!'

With a little more time I would have beefed up my story, I know that now.

The door stayed where it was.

'No can do,' a voice said. It sounded old and cranky. 'I have my hands full with a young guy here. He fell in the creek.'

'Please!' I begged, trying to get a look inside.

'Don't know if he's alive or dead,' the old man said. 'Can't get a pulse or nothing, but I think he's breathing.'

The door was closing in my face. 'Let me look!' I said. 'I trained in first aid. Maybe I can help.'

It got me inside, but Hunter was out there, still helpless. I needed to think fast if I was going to get Hunter hooked up with Lee.

Then my plans fell apart.

Lee lay on his back on a couch that doubled as the old guy's bed. At first glance you would say it was a corpse for sure – his face ghastly white, his mouth open, eyes closed. One arm hung limply off the side of the couch.

We were too late – I felt my heart thud.

Then Lee moved. He turned his head towards me. I think he recognized me.

'Go ahead – check him out,' the old guy urged. There was an open whisky bottle on the table. I smelled the alcohol on his breath.

Thud and then a rapid thump-thump-thump. My heart was racing as I crouched down by Lee's side. His eyes wouldn't focus. I thought he didn't know me after all. 'It's me – Darina,' I whispered.

'Darina. Tell Hunter I'm sorry.' His voice came out as a whisper, so slurred that I could hardly make it out.

'What did he say?' the old fisherman demanded, leaning over us with his lined, whiskery face and whisky breath.

'I'm going to get you out of here,' I leaned forward and promised Lee. *Too late!* My mind told the truth and my

183

heart went wild inside my chest.

Lee Stone was one of the Beautiful Dead *revenants* who would never find out the circumstance surrounding his passing. The storm had caught him and drained him of all his supernatural strength so that now he looked like the corpse he really was, head back against the grimy pillow, one arm hanging limp. Where were those wings and death-heads, the force field that protected him? What could even Hunter do now?

Nothing. I knew the answer without having to speak it out loud.

'No, it's me who's sorry, Lee,' I cried. Confused, the old guy backed off. 'Hunter tried to save you. He did everything he could.'

Lee's eyes showed that he'd heard me, but now he was too weak to talk. I took his cold hand and as I closed my fingers around it I saw crimson blood running down his arm from a wound on his shoulder – sticky and already congealing even though it had only just appeared. And there was more blood oozing from his ribs and a thin trickle from the corner of his mouth.

I held his hand tight. Behind us the door flew open. A strong wind gusted and when it blew itself out, Lee had gone.

* * *

184

Lee's weird half-life/half-death slowed to nothing but for those of us left it raced on. Gently I laid his lifeless arm across his chest. The fisherman stood without speaking as what happens to the Beautiful Dead when they finally leave took place. First Lee's eyelids flickered closed, the oozing blood faded. Then the light appeared – a silver glimmer surrounding the corpse, and wings beating, not fierce and wild, but soft. The glow was like a halo, slowly penetrating Lee's whole body, dissolving it and making it glisten until gradually he disappeared. Lee's would-be rescuer stared at an empty couch.

'You drank too much whisky,' I told the old fisherman harshly, leaving him to his confusion. Let this be another of the weird rumours to creep out of the mountains down into the Ellerton bars and diners. A night of bad storms, a drunken man's tale . . .

I quit the shack to look for Hunter. I called his name along the dirt track, then down by the creek. I heard only the water rushing over boulders, felt the black current race at my feet.

I sat down on the ground. 'We were too late,' I murmured.

The only answer I got was the wild beating of wings, gathering over Foxton Ridge and sweeping into the valley, and a horde of death-heads in the darkness, gleaming yellowish-white, the domes of their skulls like smooth pebbles on a shore, their eye sockets black and fathomless.

Sadness weighed me down. I'd held Lee's hand and watched him leave for ever. Now Hunter was gone too – a shadow of himself, so weak that he might not make it out of the far side to a safe haven beyond the storm.

Lightning flashed. Thunder cracked. I sat by the creek and wept.

Dawn came and I was making my way up to the ridge, empty and aching, my hopes sunk lower than ever before. I walked to the water tower overlooking the barn then plunged down the hill, half running, stumbling, longing for the Beautiful Dead to come back to the far side.

The sky glowed pink, streaked with wispy blue-grey clouds. Water drops fell from the aspen branches, puddling on the gravel earth. As the sun rose, I watched steam rise from the barn roof.

So where are you? I asked Phoenix, Hunter, Arizona and the rest.

I thought back to a time before, when another storm had forced the Beautiful Dead to flee. I'd sat through the night, waiting for them to return, and it had been longer than I'd expected – a half day for them to rest up and gather their strength, ready to make it back to the far side.

'And this is Thursday already,' I said out loud. This was serious time pressure and it weighed heavily on my shoulders. 'OK – here's the deal!'

I followed my gut feeling that I had hours to fill and it was best not to waste them hanging out there. So I headed back up to the ridge, along the deer track on to the dirt road where I hoped to hitch a ride. It was twenty minutes before the first vehicle showed up. The driver slowed to take a good long look at my drowned-rat appearance.

'You need a ride?' he said.

'To Ellerton.' I didn't care that he thought I was a homeless freak caught out by last night's storm. I climbed into the cab of his truck.

'What happened to you?'

'My car got flooded out. I ended in a gulley.'

'You live in Ellerton?'

I nodded. *OK, so you're giving me a ride but I don't need to give you my life story.*

'How old are you?'

'Twenty,' I lied.

We swung off the dirt road on to the highway. 'Did you spend the whole night on the mountain?'

'Yeah.'

'You couldn't call anyone?'

'No credit on my phone.' I sank down into the seat and closed my eyes to look like I was sleeping.

We cruised past Turkey Shoot Ridge into Centennial.

'You can drop me here,' I said. I don't remember if I even said thanks as the guy pulled up and I walked away.

I got no more than twenty paces down the street before Arizona stepped out from behind a parked car.

'Before you launch into anything, let me speak,' she said. Her green eyes flashed with impatience. 'We know what happened to Lee.'

'Hunter and I – we tried. Hunter risked everything.'

'I know. Lee was a good kid, that's why. The Beautiful Dead will miss him. Hunter's taking it badly – he figures he let him down.'

'Hunter made it back to limbo?' I asked anxiously.

'Yeah, he's safe with the others. They'll rest up and be here by midday.'

'You came alone?' I walked down the street with her, knowing it was a risk. 'What happens if someone sees you?'

Arizona pointed to the houses with their blinds still drawn, their doors locked. 'Everyone's still asleep. You and I – we need to talk.'

'I'm on my way to Westra – to your folks' house. We don't have much time.'

She nodded. 'No one knows that better than me. We have exactly thirty hours and fifteen minutes before my time is up. Which is why Hunter permitted me to return early.'

'Things have changed. These days he must trust you one hundred per cent,' I murmured, still edgy about the fact that we were on view. I pulled Arizona into an alley down the side of a small block of apartments. 'I don't know why he should do that, after the way you acted.'

She shrugged me off. 'What do you know, Darina? Honestly – I mean, what do you *really* know?'

Where did I begin? 'I know you didn't tell me about Kyle Keppler and Sable Jackson, or your kid brother. How am I supposed to help you if you hide stuff like that?'

She closed her eyes and sighed. 'Do you know what it's like when you need to protect someone you love?'

'Yeah – you put them first, above everything else. And I understand that about Raven – the poor kid needs all the care he can get. But Kyle – he's different.'

'You mean, he can take care of himself?' she muttered.

I remembered Kyle Keppler spinning his truck around, driving towards me, pulling me out of my car and dumping me in the ditch. 'Jesus, Arizona, the guy's an animal.'

Leaning against the brick wall, she looked at me through half-closed eyes. 'You know, that's what people say about the Rohrs – Brandon and Phoenix.'

'No way. You can't make that comparison!'

She overrode me with one of those old, arrogant flicks of her wrist. 'They say Brandon can only settle an argument with his fists, and Phoenix took after his brother.'

'You know that's not true.'

'But it's how it looks from the outside – that's what we're talking about here.'

'Are you saying that Kyle is like Phoenix?' I was fired up and ready to walk away, to leave Arizona to her Beautiful Dead fate and never speak to her again. 'Phoenix didn't cheat on me, remember.'

She gave a small nod. 'And if he had, would you still love him?'

I took a sharp breath, unable to give an answer that didn't hack the legs from under my own argument.

'You see – you don't stop having feelings for someone, even when they hurt you. You hang on in and hope it will go away.'

'But Sable was pregnant, they were going to

get married . . .'

'I know – don't tell me. I *should*'ve walked away. I did try.'

For a long time I stood in silence, shaking my head. 'What about Kyle? After you knew the full story about Sable and the baby, did he finish it with you on the spot?'

'He tried to. But he was like me – he couldn't help himself. He would back off for a few days but then he would call me again.'

'Saying he still loved you?'

She nodded. 'And I would go around to Mike's Motors to see him. Other guys – Brandon, Jon Jackson – might be there and I would have to make some excuse.'

I pictured the dirty looks and sly comments flying in Arizona's direction. 'You know something – that wasn't love, it was masochism.'

'An obsession,' she sighed. 'But I saw a side of Kyle you wouldn't believe. Not scary, but funny. He goofs around and makes me feel good about myself . . . He *did*,' she corrected herself. 'He understood the way my mind worked. With him I could be myself.'

'That's really sad,' I told her. 'You couldn't be yourself with anyone except Kyle. I get it now. At least, I think I do.'

'So you see why Kyle needs you to stay away from

Forest Lake – to keep his relationship with Sable and his kid,' Arizona stated. 'The only time he ever got mad with me was when I showed up at his house.'

'That's crazy. Why did you do that?' The old saying about pots and kettles might spring to mind. I mean, hadn't I done exactly that?

'To sit quietly in my car and watch. I wasn't about to walk in on him and Sable – I just wanted to see them together, maybe convince myself that it was over between Kyle and me.'

'But he spotted you?'

She nodded. 'He didn't touch me or lose it with me, but he said never, never to do that again. And now I want you to promise me the same thing.'

'What exactly?' I didn't see that Arizona was in a position to lay down conditions.

'To leave Sable out of it, and Kyle.'

'Even though he was one of the last people you saw before you ended up in Hartmann?'

She shook her head fiercely. 'I don't know that for sure. The last thing I remember was driving to the mall. I have no idea if I made it to Mike's Motors, or if Kyle was even there.'

I gave up on the questions, knowing we could never get beyond Arizona's memory block. 'So you're

OK with me going over to your family's house?'

'To do what?'

Honestly, you'd have thought I was sleeping with the enemy, the way she reacted. 'To talk with whoever's there – with Peter. Or maybe Frank will give me some new details to work on.'

'Or maybe not.' She laughed the old Arizona laugh – scoffing and humourless. 'Getting information from my father is a blood-from-a-stone activity.'

'I noticed.' I didn't get time to ask how come that was true before a window above our heads opened and a woman leaned out.

'Quit that yakkety-yakking at this time in the morning,' she yelled down.

Arizona and I reacted as if we'd been stung by a swarm of hornets. We got out of that alleyway and back on the street.

'So go ahead – talk to my grandfather again,' she told me, getting ready to dematerialize.

'Where will you be?' I asked.

'Around,' she told me. 'You won't see me, but I'll definitely be there.'

I went straight to Logan's house and knocked on his door.

Though it was only 8.00 a.m. he appeared, fully

dressed and alert. 'Hey, Darina, what's up?'

'My car got wrecked,' I said feebly. 'And before you ask – no, it wasn't down to me. A rock flew up and smashed the hood.'

'So you want a ride to school?'

'Not this morning, thanks. But can you drive me over to Westra?' To stop him asking more questions, I put in what sounded like a genuine reason. 'You remember the woman who fell off her horse? Her husband is Peter Hall – he works out there.'

'And you want to ask how she's doing?' Quickly Logan grabbed his keys. 'Sure, I'll swing by there for you.'

I smiled and sat beside him. We drove without a lot of conversation, just easy and relaxed as far as he knew. At the end of North 22 Street, I asked for him to set me down.

'You want me to wait?' he asked.

'No – I'll walk back.' I gave him a grateful smile and watched him colour up. *How come I don't fall in love with the easy-to-read nice guys of this world?* I asked myself, not for the first time.

As Logan turned his car in the direction of Ellerton High and I walked the half-mile to number 2850, I couldn't help glancing over my shoulder to look for the invisible Arizona. How weird – she was coming back to visit her house a year after she died and only I knew.

I turned in the drive and headed towards the gardener's annexe, but before I'd gone far I saw Raven sitting in his usual spot in the summer house. He looked up from his sketch pad then quickly down again. For a few seconds, I heard Arizona's startled, helpless reaction in a little gust of wind, like a sigh through the redwood trees by the gate.

Soon Peter Hall walked out of his potting-shed and cut across the lawn to meet me.

'How come Raven's home from school?' I asked. 'The last I heard, he was back at the Institute.'

'Thanks to you, I hear.' The old man steered me away from Raven towards his annexe. 'The principal gave Frank a description of the girl who found him – tall, skinny, with short, dark hair – we figured it might be you.'

'You know me – I like to drive in the mountains,' I shrugged. 'So have they taken him out of school?'

'Finally,' Peter sighed. 'I guess he ran away one too many times. Rebecca Davis and Allyson talked it through – everyone decided he should take a break from the Institute.'

There was more agitation among the branches of the fir trees – Arizona finding it real hard to see her kid brother and hear this latest piece of news yet not be able to walk up to him, put her arm around his shoulders, go through a few Warhol prints with him and make his blank eyes light up.

'You know something else?' Peter went on. 'Frank finally left home last night.'

'They're going ahead with the divorce?'

'For sure. He moved into Jenna's and my place.'

'Wow, that's big,' I realized.

Peter nodded. 'Like a house of cards collapsing. Raven comes home. Frank leaves. And today for the first time in her life, Allyson cuts work.'

'She's home?' I looked in alarm at the big house with its open front door and a dozen blank windows glinting in the cold sun. 'And what about you, Peter? Where do you and Jenna stand now?'

'We're still history,' he said, gesturing towards the cardboard boxes on the floor. He'd stacked his gardening books inside, along with his kettle and coffee cups. 'Now that Frank's off the scene, Allyson says she doesn't want us to visit Raven – she'll hire a professional carer instead.'

'She's cutting you out?' When I'm shocked, I have a bad habit of stating the obvious.

Peter hunched his shoulders. 'Unless she changes her mind,' he muttered. 'But I know Allyson – she never goes back on her word. The fact is – we're out of here for good.'

'Darina, you have to go back in and talk to Raven – help him to get through this!' When I met up with Arizona outside the gates to her house, she was a mess. She'd overheard every word of the conversation between me and her grandfather and she couldn't bear for me to walk away.

'Why? What good will it do?'

'Talk about his sketches, try telling him about me – why I'm not around any more, how I didn't leave him because I wanted to. No, forget that. Just tell him I love him.'

The force of her plea nearly knocked me over, yet I remembered Phoenix telling me Raven's autistic brain was wired differently, so he was impossible to reach. 'He won't understand,' I told her. 'You know that better than I do.'

Arizona looked at me in total despair. 'Try,' she begged. 'You know it's the only thing I care about – that Raven realizes I would have done anything for him. He's an amazing, special kid. Tell him that from me, Darina.'

'I don't think this is a good idea,' I muttered. I didn't even know if I could get back into the garden without being seen, but luckily Peter had vanished from the annexe and there was no sign of life in the big house either.

So I went back into the garden and crept up on the kid, catching him by surprise.

You'd think I was pointing a gun in his face, the way he reacted with a big jolt of shock running through his whole body.

'It's OK,' I murmured. 'Remember me, Raven? We met a couple of times before.'

He clutched his sketch book to his chest and started to rock back and forth, refusing to look at me. Poor kid – skinny and fragile as a bird, with that black, glossy hair and eyes that darted here and there.

'Show me what you just drew.'

But no – he kept the sketches hidden and he rocked more rapidly.

'I won't hurt you – I'm your friend,' I tried to tell him, but I wasn't getting anywhere. Hadn't I lied to him and dumped him with the school principal?

'Raven, I knew your sister, Arizona.'

Her name was the one thing that broke down the barrier. I said 'Arizona' and before the word fell from my lips, the kid had stopped rocking and was looking hungrily at me, wanting more.

'Yeah, Arizona – she told me about you, Raven. "He

draws the best pictures", is what she said. Do you want to show me your book?'

His eyes widened. He looked from me to the sketch pad then suddenly thrust it towards me.

I took it and started to turn the pages. 'Hey, this is your house, and this is the summer house – how neat is that. And Peter's annexe, and this is your school.' Pretty soon we were sitting side by side on the summer house bench, heads bent over the sketch book, tracing the images with our fingers. I turned another page and found myself staring at a portrait of Arizona. It was totally her – I was drawn to the almond-shaped eyes and the arched eyebrows, the long, oval face framed by straight black hair. 'You drew this?' I asked.

Raven ran his forefinger around the shape of the face, touching it lightly and tenderly. Then he looked up at me with the ghost of a smile.

I was smiling back at him, trying to hold back the tears when Allyson Taylor, alias Monster Mom, interrupted us. 'I don't know who you are or what you're doing here,' she said coldly. 'But you should leave before I call the cops.'

'There's no need, I'm out of here,' I told her. I stood up, surprised to feel Raven catch hold of the bottom of my jacket and refuse to let go. Another surprise was the way

Allyson looked without her TV face – pale and drawn, with her fair hair pulled back, her mouth sagging at the corners and bags under her eyes. 'I came to see Peter,' I explained. 'I was the one who found Jenna on the mountain after her accident.'

'So did you see him before he left?' Allyson's gaze had fixed on Raven's hand clutching my jacket.

I nodded. 'And your son showed me his sketches. He has a real talent.'

'He likes to draw.' There was a break in the frosty tone. 'Let go of the jacket, Raven, be a good kid.'

He turned his head away but held on tight.

'It's OK, it's not a problem.'

'Let go – please!' Allyson reached out and tried to uncurl his fingers. There was something so sad and hopeless about the action that it brought on the tears. 'I'm sorry,' she sobbed, stepping back and covering her face with her hand.

'No problem – honestly. Arizona talked to me about her brother. I understand.'

'She did?' Allyson found this piece of information hard to swallow. 'I didn't think Arizona confided in people. I thought she suffered from the family trait of bottling stuff up, big style.'

'Most of the time she did,' I agreed. I was staring at the

weeping woman, wondering where Monster Mom and my Suspect Number Two had gone. 'But some things are just too hard to hide.'

Allyson came inside the summer house again and we all sat down, Raven still holding tight to me. 'So she explained his condition?'

Right then the sense of Arizona grew stronger. I heard her voice saying over and over, *You won't see me but I'll definitely be there.*

'Arizona said Raven was an amazing, special boy,' I told them both. 'She wouldn't have wanted to leave you, Raven, because she loved you more than anything in the world.'

'Don't – he doesn't understand.' Tears ran down Allyson's cheeks. 'He thinks his sister is going to come back. Every day he waits for her.'

'Maybe you do understand, Raven. You know that Arizona loves you.'

'So why did she do what she did?' A bitter tone came through Allyson's tears. 'If she loved him, she wouldn't have drowned herself in the lake.'

I took a deep breath. 'Maybe that's not the way it happened?'

'Sure it was,' came the defensive reply. 'Suicide by drowning. That's what they said at the inquest – no question.'

'And how come everyone is so sure?'

'Because there's no other way of looking at it.' Allyson raised her hand to stroke Raven's hair back from his face. 'Anyway, the family – Frank's family – has a history. His uncle blew his own brains out. He has a brother with bi-polar disorder.'

'I'm sorry. I didn't know that.' Suddenly my own single-parent, no-money family situation began to look kind of desirable.

'And Frank was affected by that, naturally. With him you don't see much emotion. He keeps things locked up. Even when Raven was born and we first knew something was wrong, Frank never shared how he felt. And I had to do all the practical stuff – the clinics, the diagnoses, the treatments – he never came along with me.'

'I'm sorry,' I said again. My view of the Taylor set-up was shifting again. Every time I thought I had a hold on it – hyper-ambitious mom unwilling to give up career to care for autistic son – the footsteps in the sand settled, the wind blew and blurred the lines so that everything looked different.

'Frank wanted reasons,' Allyson sighed. 'Is Raven the way he is due to genetic factors? Abnormal levels of serotonin in the brain, a virus during pregnancy, Fragile X Syndrome – he went through everything.'

'It didn't help?'

'No, though when she grew older, that's what Arizona did too. She read all the theories, just like her dad.'

'She was smart,' I reminded her.

'But it led to fights between us. She always thought she knew the answers – a special diet, cognitive behavioural therapy . . .'

'I hear you.'

'So I was the bad guy, going down the conventional route and sending Raven away to the Lindsey Institute, and when he was home making sure he took his seizure medication. We fought over that a lot, while Frank – he did his usual thing of withdrawing.'

'Leaving you to deal with the practicalities?'

Allyson nodded. 'You're young, so you can't know what it's like to be married, but not have someone you can rely on, someone who is offering you support. It makes a person bitter.'

I thought my way into her situation and agreed.

'You know something – soon after we lost Arizona, Frank took away all the pictures of her, plus her school books, her jewellery, her clothes – everything.'

'What did he do with them?'

'He stored them in boxes and locked them in the annexe, said he didn't want to be reminded. That's how he dealt with it.' Allyson breathed in deeply, then pulled her shoulders back. 'Peter told you that everything around here changed? Raven gets to take a break from the Institute while Frank and I take a break from each other.'

I nodded. Now she really was flying solo for real, and it showed in her red-rimmed eyes, her drooping mouth. I did what I would have believed was impossible thirty minutes earlier – I felt truly, deeply sorry for Allyson Taylor.

So where was Arizona when I came out on to the street?

I checked in both directions, then set off for town, guessing that by now the Beautiful Dead had arrived back at Foxton and that Hunter had ordered her to meet with them – which meant that I had to return there too.

'This is when possession of a superpower would come in useful,' I muttered as I hurried along. 'A quick fix of dematerialization is what I need right now.' Otherwise, how did I get up to the ridge?

Through Brandon, that was how. He came by on his Harley, just as I reached the industrial unit behind the shopping mall. 'Kyle fixed your car,' he told me, stopping at the edge of the sidewalk. He looked amused by the fact that I was having to get from A to B on foot.

I stared back hard. 'Kyle?' I echoed.

'Sure. No charge. I told him it was the least he could do.'

'Did he . . . did he say anything?'

'Only that you needed to learn to stop poking your nose in where it isn't wanted. I didn't ask.' Patting the pillion seat, Brandon told me to hop on the bike. 'Come on – do you want to get your car back or not?'

Of course I did. But I wasn't happy riding pillion with Brandon Rohr, putting my arms around his waist and feeling the warmth of his body beneath his white T-shirt. It made me want to cry.

We rode by the electrical wholesalers unit, took a left and headed for Mike's Motors. Brandon pulled up outside the workshop, telling me to wait by the Dyna while he went inside. A couple of minutes later he drove my car down the ramp. 'Good as new,' he said, getting out and throwing me the keys.

In the workshop doorway I saw Kyle Keppler standing with his arms folded, watching intently.

'How did you do that?' I muttered to Brandon in disbelief.

'Kyle knows he was out of line. Besides, he owes me a couple of favours.'

'So thanks,' I nodded. I was about to get into the car

and drive away when Brandon put his hand on my shoulder and stopped me.

'Crazy,' he mumbled, staring into my eyes. 'I swore to my brother that I'd take care of you.'

The heavy hand made me uncomfortable and feel all the differences between Brandon and my own Phoenix.

'Thanks,' I said again. 'You're doing a good job.'

Brandon let out a sigh. 'Do you think Phoenix knows it – wherever he is now?'

9

Wherever he is now. Like I said already – sometimes people tread so hard on my secret that I want to scream. I drove fast up to Foxton, desperate to see Phoenix and looking at storm damage by the roadside. In the burn-out area by Turkey Shoot, charred trees had toppled and lay criss-crossed on the hillsides, while torrents of brown, foaming water flooded the gulleys. Swinging left at the Foxton junction, I hurried past the fisherman's shack where Lee had made his exit.

High on the ridge, where the track ended, I abandoned my car and ran along the deer track towards the water tower.

Phoenix, I need to see you! My heart cried out, my body was blasted by the high wind that had blown the storm out a few hours earlier. Wind and wings mixed together, the sound rising to a fresh tempest as I paused by the rusting tower. Any stranger facing this invisible force field would surely have turned back.

But I ducked my head and held my jacket tight across my chest, plunging down the hill towards the dripping, steaming barn. I ran blind, head down, heart thumping – right into my boyfriend's arms.

'Darina, it's OK,' Phoenix whispered, his lips against the top of my head. Then, putting one hand under my chin, he tilted my head until I was looking into his eyes.

'Oh God, I was scared you wouldn't make it through the storm!' I cried, clutching the lapels of his leather jacket like it was a matter of life and death.

'I'm here,' he soothed – his voice low and intense, waiting for me to calm down. The wild wind blew through his hair, pushing it across his forehead, then flicking it back from his beautiful face.

'Lee . . .' I mumbled, hiding my face against his chest.

'I know. Poor baby, poor Darina – I'm sorry you saw that.'

'There was blood. He was in pain. There was no way I could help.'

'Hunter told us,' Phoenix said softly. 'Lee took a direct hit – a fork of lightning hit him full on.'

'I tried to get him out of the shack,' I sobbed. 'Then Hunter could have helped him.'

'No. It was already too late. We don't survive long after a direct hit. We fade within a couple of hours.' Phoenix wanted to make me feel better. He held me tight and stroked my hair. 'Lee was too weak, the electric storm had done its work before you got there.'

'It's so sad.' Gradually I was able to stop crying and relax into Phoenix's strong arms. 'It scared me real bad.'

'Poor Darina,' he said again, squeezing me and rocking me gently as we stood in the yard. 'This is tough for you.'

I shook my head. 'No, this isn't about me. What really scared me was the idea that the same thing could happen to any of you – Summer, Arizona, especially you, Phoenix.'

This time there were no comforting words. He looked into my eyes without denying it.

'A storm can happen any time. Last night, you were in Ellerton with me. It could have been you as well as Lee.'

Phoenix nodded. 'We all take that risk. That's why Hunter sends us out in twos or threes whenever he can.'

'That guy is seriously brave,' I confided.

Phoenix smiled. 'So you don't hate him any more?'

'Yeah, I still do. He's way too controlling.' I managed to grin back at him. 'He's like the worst kind of father – the kind you can't argue with.'

'Tell me about it.' If anyone knew this about their

overlord, it was my boyfriend and the other members of the Beautiful Dead. 'You know he's listening right now?'

I nodded. 'Where is he?'

'In the hayloft with the others. Are you ready to join them?' Taking my hand, Phoenix led me into the barn. He bolted the door behind us.

Out of the wind at last, and calmer now, I raised my head and took a look around. Old, dust-covered bridles and reins hung from their hooks, spades and forks rested against the walls. Dusty spiders' webs were slung from beam to beam, undisturbed.

'Upstairs,' Phoenix prompted. Again he led the way. The wooden steps creaked under his weight.

And there they were – Arizona, Summer, Eve with her baby, Kori, Donna and Iceman – the Beautiful Dead. And their overlord, Hunter, stern-faced and powerful.

They looked remote and serious, deep in grief over Lee.

Arizona came over. 'Sorry Hunter made me leave earlier. But you carried on speaking with Raven?' she asked anxiously.

I nodded. 'I told him everything you asked me to.'

She drank in my words, as if every strand of hope, delicate as the spiders' webs, hung on my reply. 'How was he?'

'I can't lie to you. Anyway, you saw him yourself. Allyson said he still expects you back.'

Panic flickered across Arizona's face. 'Allyson?' she echoed.

'She showed up. And she confirmed that she doesn't want your grandparents to visit any more. She's definitely taking the paid-carer route.'

'My God, she can't do that!' My answer threw Arizona into a tailspin. 'Raven needs his family around him.'

'I'm sorry. But to me, Allyson didn't come across the way I expected.' I tried to settle her panic. 'She does care for Raven – more than I thought.'

'Yeah, she cares enough to put him in that school! She cares enough not to look at stuff like diet and toxins, modern therapies!'

'That wasn't what I got from her,' was all I could say, turning to Hunter who had joined us. 'None of this is how it looks from the outside.'

'Including Arizona,' the overlord pointed out. 'You never expected her to be suffering the way she does.'

'True. Listen, Arizona, I won't walk away from Raven – whatever happens.'

'You swear?' She caught on to this like a lifebelt thrown to a man fallen overboard. 'You'll be a link with his past. You won't let him forget me?'

'I promise. He knew your name and he connects me with you. I did what you asked – I told him you loved him.'

I guess at this point Arizona would have been happy to make her exit. She was where she wanted to be – knowing that in future I would look out for Raven, that he understood a little and she had done everything she could. I genuinely believe she didn't care how she'd died or what happened to her now.

But the Beautiful Dead had a mission to get to the core of the mystery, and Hunter was the guy who was in control.

'We have less than twenty-four hours,' he reminded us. 'It's still looking like a suicide, unless Darina can come up with something else.'

Everyone stared at me.

'Let's get moving.' Summer broke into the tense mood. 'What have we got, Darina? We have a boyfriend who's living on a knife-edge in case Sable finds out about his affair with Arizona. We have the Taylor family so caught up in fights and arguments that no one can think straight.'

'Plus, grandparents who care, but are kept at arm's length,' I added. 'And a kid brother who runs away from his school on the same morning that Arizona drowns.'

'And me,' Arizona reminded us. 'One crazy, mixed-up girl who has no friend or family she can talk to. Maybe that's it – I gave way to the pressure and jumped in that lake, like they said.'

Summer did something I'd never seen before – she grew angry. 'You don't really believe that!' she cried, getting into Arizona's face. 'You're a fighter. You don't do surrender!'

Arizona shook her head. 'Maybe I did – just that once.'

'I don't believe it.' I agreed with Summer. 'Even if the Kyle situation was hopeless and it was getting to you, you'd never have given up on Raven. No, somebody else was involved and you've blocked it out – like the trauma is too strong.'

'So Darina, you should go back to Ellerton,' Hunter broke in. 'Phoenix can go with you. If you decide to meet Kyle Keppler face to face and ask him exactly where he was and who he saw the day Arizona died, Phoenix can take care of you.'

If Kyle came across with the violence, Phoenix could zap him with his super-strength again. He could get me out of any danger I might find myself in. I also knew this was not a tactic Hunter would favour in anything except an emergency. Time was agonizingly short and the main questions were still unanswered.

I turned to Phoenix and saw that he was scared on my behalf. 'Hey, at least we get to spend another night together,' I joked.

Arizona didn't appreciate my humour. 'You won't get any answers from Kyle,' she still insisted. 'No way was he involved.'

We didn't believe her – our silence said it all.

We were in the hayloft and our guard was down. Otherwise we would have heard the bikes gathering by Angel Rock.

They'd come up from Forest Lake, ghost-busting on their Harleys and Kawasakis, a group of tough guys who had listened to the ramblings of an old fisherman who had found his way down from his shack with an incoherent tale of a kid who got caught in the storm, who drowned in the creek, and whose bleeding corpse glittered and disappeared in front of his eyes.

At first they'd laughed at the crazy old man then they'd drunk a couple of beers. After that, someone suggested they ride up and take another look.

'Iceman, get up there!' Hunter ordered when he did finally pick up the sound of engines. 'Donna, you go with him. Set up a barrier – don't let anyone through.'

The commands came thick and fast. He told Summer, Eve and Arizona to circle round the back of the bikers and then approach from the direction of Amos Peak. 'We squeeze them from all sides,' he explained. 'We bunch them together, then we push them along the ridge towards Foxton. Do whatever you have to do!' He told Phoenix and me not to move from the house until the coast was clear. 'Go!' he ordered, half pushing us down the steps. 'Lock the door from the inside.'

We obeyed, crossing the yard as the Beautiful Dead spread out across the hillside, disappearing into the aspens as dusk began to fall. They moved silently and swiftly, like shadows.

'Hunter's got a crazy look,' Phoenix told me as we went into the house. 'He's mad that he didn't post lookouts. Now we're all in danger.'

'Even Hunter gets it wrong sometimes,' I shrugged. I felt safe in the house, though the walls were only rough-sawn logs and the iron bolt on the door was rusty. I was happy that Hunter had chosen Phoenix to stay and take care of me. 'So you have to tell me what's happening up at Angel Rock,' I insisted.

Phoenix listened hard. 'Donna and Iceman are in position. The bikers are talking amongst themselves.'

'You can hear them?' Personally I could only pick up natural sounds of wind rustling through dry grass, of breeze shaking the fall leaves in the aspens. 'Do we know who's there?'

'I can tell you how many, but not who they are. Iceman's saying maybe twelve or thirteen. He and Donna are starting to drive them along the ridge. Arizona and the others will soon be behind them, piling on the pressure.'

'I hope they leave without a fight,' I shivered. I wasn't so comfortable now that the light had faded and I knew we couldn't light any lamps that would give away our presence. We sat in the dark, waiting.

'It's working – they're riding away,' Phoenix reported. 'Once we set up the barriers, they're not so tough.'

I pictured panic spreading amongst the bikers, rising from uneasy jitters as the invisible wings began to beat, to a jolting fear as the death-heads began to swoop, and then a crazy mindlessness. For all their beer-fuelled bravado, they would crouch low over their handlebars, turn up their engines and ride the hell out.

'Two have broken free of the group,' Phoenix told me uneasily. He went to the window to gaze up at the ridge. 'You hear that? They turned back in this direction.'

'Are you certain?'

'Iceman is coming after them. You can hear them now, can't you?'

Joining Phoenix at the window, I listened hard until I picked up the whine of two engines. I stared up at the black hillside, my heart in my mouth.

'This is serious,' Phoenix decided. 'They're way ahead of Iceman – I don't think he can head them off.'

Suddenly two bright lights appeared on the ridge, their beams dipping into hollows, then raking up into the dark sky. 'What do we do now?' I asked.

'You wait here. I'll go help Iceman.'

'But Hunter said for you to stay here!'

'No, you – *you* have to stay hidden,' he insisted. 'Keep the door bolted. You'll be OK.' Phoenix slid the bolt then stepped out on to the porch. 'Close the door, Darina!'

I clenched my teeth and forced the bolt back in place. Then I stood with my shoulder to the door, eyes closed and hardly able to breathe. The two bikes raced into the valley, yellow headlamps invading the blackness.

Out in the yard, Phoenix saw a way to stop them. He seized a roll of fencing wire stored by the side of the barn, raised it over his head and tossed it in the path of the nearest bike. The rider braked and skidded, making a sharp swerve across the track of the second rider. The two bikes collided and both men fell to the ground. Through the grimy window I saw them land in the dirt. The next moment, Iceman had joined Phoenix by the barn.

Two Beautiful Dead versus two no-brain bikers from Forest Lake – it should have been no contest. I expected

Phoenix and Iceman to move in and toss the two guys aside like garbage, zap their minds clean, then send them home with sore heads.

But that wasn't what happened. In the low beam of one of the headlights I saw the first rider struggle to his feet and lurch towards the house. Meanwhile, his buddy had totally lost it. He picked up the roll of razor wire and flung it back at Iceman and Phoenix. The wire unwound at their feet in a snaking, lethal coil. Now the first guy was blundering on to the porch, reeling against the cabin wall to catch his breath. I saw him close up and recognized his features even in the dark. It was Kyle Keppler – who else?

Fresh panic washed over me. and I went weak at the knees. Phoenix and Iceman were trapped, the guy I suspected of killing Arizona was less than a metre away, coming around from the shock of being thrown from his bike and looking for a weapon to use against his attackers. He picked up a long-handled axe that leaned against the wall.

'Phoenix!' I screamed a warning from inside the house. My face was at the window, plain to see.

Keppler heard and saw. Instead of running at the original enemy, he suddenly turned the axe on the door, raising it and bringing it crashing down, splintering the wood and smashing the glass into a thousand pieces. Another blow smashed clean through the bolt and the door swung open. 'Here, Jonno – catch this!' he yelled at the second guy, tossing the axe through the air like a tomahawk.

Jonno . . . Jon . . . Jon Jackson, Kyle's joined-at-the-hip brother-in-law. Jackson caught the weapon and forced Phoenix and Iceman back towards the barn.

Which left me facing Kyle Keppler alone in the dark. Terror grabbed me and fixed me to the spot. In my own mind, I was dead – no question.

'This is it, girl. You got in my way one too many times.' He blocked the doorway, his feet crunched over the shattered glass. 'Whatever is happening here, you're at the heart of it.'

'Nothing's happening,' I protested. 'A few kids from Ellerton High and me – we hang out up here once in a while.' I fell back against the stove as Kyle towered over me.

He grabbed my wrist and swung me back into the middle of the room. 'These would be the same kids who tossed the fencing wire across the yard? They're going to be sorry they did that.'

I closed my eyes and prayed that Jon Jackson wasn't as good with the axe as Keppler had been. Phoenix and

Iceman would handle him eventually, but it would take time.

'So what really happens out here?' Still gripping my wrist, Keppler sat me down in a chair by the table. 'I hear a kid drowned in the creek last night. Who was he? Where's the corpse?'

'I don't know. Don't ask me!' I cowered as Keppler raised his hand against me. I really was dead, unless Phoenix came soon. 'Arizona used to come here,' I told him.

Speaking her name acted as a brake. The raised fist didn't come crashing down.

'No one knew about this place back then. She liked the silence.'

'Arizona was here?' Keppler tried to make it compute as he glanced around the ancient room. I noticed that this time he didn't try to deny the relationship. 'When was that? She didn't tell me.'

'Typical Arizona – she liked to keep secrets,' I reminded him.

'But she told you?'

'We used to talk a lot.'

'About me?'

I nodded. 'She said she loved you. She tried to break free but she wasn't strong enough.'

A disbelieving half-smile crept across Kyle's face. 'Are

we talking about the same girl? I never met a person stronger than Arizona.'

'On the outside,' I agreed. 'You don't have any idea how much she was hurting on the inside.'

He took a long look at me in the moonlit room, converting my last comment into a harsh criticism of himself. 'She made her choice,' he argued.

I met his gaze. 'She was seventeen.'

Something snapped inside his head. He went back to being psycho-man, leaning in so close that I could feel his breath on my face. 'What do you know?' he snarled, unconsciously echoing his dead ex-girlfriend. 'What do you *really* know?'

Hunter found us like that – face to face, me helpless, Kyle Keppler jerking me from the kitchen chair, about to smash the back of his hand against my face. The overlord went in for the kill. In an instant he shrivelled Keppler's strength to less than a baby, making him stagger back and sink to his knees. Another mind-zap sent him sprawling full length, clutching his head and yelling out in pain. Hunter stood over him, calm and impassive, listening to him howl. 'Don't move from this room,' he told me quietly.

I'd been thinking of running out into the yard, and Hunter knew it.

'Phoenix and Iceman have dealt with Jackson,' he told me. 'He's already on his way out of here.'

True – I heard the whine of a Harley engine and saw a single beam of light rake across the hillside.

'You talked to Keppler about Arizona,' Hunter remarked. 'That was risky.'

'I had to say something. He was so angry – I thought he was going to kill me.'

Hunter blinked, then turned his cold grey eyes on me. 'You need to trust me, Darina. Keppler is nothing I can't handle.'

'But I didn't know where you were!' I cried. 'I thought you were on the ridge with the others.'

'I'm everywhere,' he said, as he hauled Keppler to his feet and gave his mind one more blast of zombie hypnosis. 'I come when I'm needed.'

Then he threw Keppler out into the yard, where Phoenix and Iceman put the brainwashed husk of a guy back on his bike and pointed him up the hill.

'So thanks,' I breathed – a word that didn't measure up to the drama of the occasion, I know.

Hunter's back was turned, he was standing in the doorway watching Keppler leave.

'That's the place – there, where you're standing now,' he told me, as if he had eyes in the back of his head.

His voice had turned spacey and distant. 'Roll back the rug, Darina.'

'What do you mean?' I stared at the floor and the faded, patterned rug.

'That's where I fell. Roll it back.'

I crouched and lifted the corner of the rug to see a dark stain on the plain boards – black in the moonlight, but no doubt crimson all those years before.

'My blood,' Hunter confirmed. 'Mentone shot me and I fell right there.'

I shivered. *Why tell me this now?*

Hunter's gestures were slow and trancelike. 'Marie was standing there, by the stove. She was in shock – paralysed by what had happened. Mentone drew his gun and fired.'

He hit you in the head, the bullet went clean through your skull – I know!

'I haven't spoken about it to anyone,' Hunter said, his voice weary. 'Year after year I return. I've seen justice done for others among the Beautiful Dead – many times. And every time a restless soul is released I know my job is done.'

'I don't understand why you're telling me this now.' Hunter seemed to have made time stand still – I was caught in his memory capsule, struggling to break out.

He turned to look at me, catching me in that powerful

gaze. 'What is it about you, Darina?' he asked. 'I tell myself you're not even like her.'

'Like Marie?' I was struggling to breathe, caught like an insect on a pin. *So what if I remind you of your wife? Don't do this to me!*

'She was a good woman – happy and easy, no dark shadows inside her head, not like you. Marie was full of life. She dressed real pretty.'

'I'm sorry you don't like the way I dress,' I muttered. 'Things were different then.'

It was as if I hadn't spoken. 'And then I look in your eyes and they're the same,' he sighed. 'The painful memories flood back. They give me no rest.'

'So how come you never found justice for yourself?' I asked. 'You help the Beautiful Dead, but never yourself.'

He focused in on my face even more. 'It's never going to happen. I won't find peace.'

'Maybe one day,' I said, without believing it or expecting him to.

He sighed again. 'Smooth down the rug, Darina. Phoenix and Iceman are waiting. Let's go.'

The Beautiful Dead came down from Foxton Ridge and gathered in the barn. They'd used up a lot of energy on the Forest Lake intruders so they sat quietly, waiting for

Hunter to make his next plan – Donna next to Eve, Iceman keeping a lookout from the hayloft, Phoenix standing guard at the door. They were all edgy, reacting to the smallest sound, exchanging uneasy glances.

'So Phoenix gets to stay the night with you in Ellerton?' Arizona checked with me. Of them all she seemed most restless and afraid.

I checked my watch and saw that it was almost midnight. 'Yeah, give me a good story for why I'm so late home.'

'For Laura?'

'You got it. Forget the one about my car running out of gas – I already used that a hundred times.'

'Say you were at Logan's house and didn't look at the time,' she suggested. 'That usually works. Keep her talking while Phoenix sneaks in.'

I agreed that it was my best shot. 'Tomorrow I pay your boyfriend one last visit,' I promised. 'I ask him outright – did you visit him at work the day you died? Did you and he drive out to Hartmann together?'

Arizona turned away impatiently. 'He'll tell you no.'

'But do I believe him?' I stepped back in front of her. 'Think again, Arizona, and think hard. Did you drive to the mall? Did you corner Kyle and beg him to leave Sable one last time?'

Anger sparked in her dark-brown eyes. 'OK, Darina – let me play it back the way you want to see it. I drive to Mike's Motors, park my car and go inside. Kyle is working. He's not happy to see me. I say, "Please leave your pregnant girlfriend, soon to be your wife, and be with me. We were made for each other – twin souls who can't be parted!" This is too much pressure and Kyle totally loses control. Maybe he has a workshop tool – something heavy – in his hand. We struggle. He hits me – an accident, or on purpose. I fall to the floor.'

'Stop it!' I begged. It felt like Arizona had moved so close to the edge that she would fall into a crazy abyss and never get her sanity back.

'You never asked to see my death mark, did you, Darina? Shall I show it to you? Would you like to see it?'

'No. Stop. If you don't remember what happened, you don't remember. I'm sorry, I didn't mean to push you this hard.'

'Death mark!' she insisted, her gaze almost as powerful as Hunter's. I felt my willpower crumble. 'You expect it to be here on my chest, showing how I fell into the water and drowned.' Her long fingers swept across her slender upper body. 'But it's not there, believe me.'

'So where?' I realized she was about to show me whether I liked it or not.

Slowly she raised both arms to lift her long hair clear of her back. She twisted it like a skein of black silk, then turned so I could see her bare neck. The skin was white, every vertebra visible and vulnerable. 'Do you see?' she whispered.

The angel-wing tattoo nestled between two bones in her neck, dark and clear against her skin, very delicate, totally definite.

'Yes,' I replied. 'You didn't drown in the lake. You broke your neck – that's what killed you.'

When I got home, Laura was past giving me a fight. She wore her wounded look – *OK, so I'm only your mother. I don't expect you to show me any consideration or respect.*

'Sorry, I didn't look at the time,' I mumbled as I sloped off towards my room.

'Jim called,' she told me. 'He had an accident. His tyre blew and he skidded off the road.'

This stopped me in my tracks. 'Is he OK?'

She nodded. 'The car got towed away. He's spending the night in a motel.'

'Are *you* OK?' Obviously not – she was pale, her eyes were red from crying.

'What is it with this family and cars?' she sighed. 'What is it with this family, period?'

'Look, he's not hurt, thank God.' By now I'd given Phoenix plenty of time to climb through my bedroom window and Jim being involved in a minor traffic accident wasn't high on my list of priorities. 'Get some sleep. It'll look OK in the morning.'

'Where have you been, Darina?' She sounded exasperated. 'Don't tell me Jordan's or Hannah's house – I already checked.'

'Logan's,' I told her, rushing up the stairs. I knew she wouldn't have called his house in case she got Logan's dad and he was drunk as usual.

Phoenix was there, waiting.

To have him in my room, filling the space with his beautiful presence, was heaven. I can never get a handle on how handsome he is, how he lights up my soul every time I see him, and how I feel safe with him even with danger all around. I fell into his arms.

Phoenix held me – I'm the centre of his world, like he is of mine. We're part of each other – no one can tear us apart.

We lay on the bed together, lost in the moment, happy in spite of everything. His face was so close, so smooth – dark eyelashes shadowed his pale grey eyes, his lips were soft against my cheek.

'What are you thinking?' he asked after the longest silence.

'Nothing. Only how perfect this is.'

'Did we finally stop the world and step off?'

'I guess so. We're out in furthest space, floating amongst the planets. It's dark and silent. No one can reach us.'

'Time stood still?'

I nodded and kissed him, softly at first, then raising myself over him and sinking into a harder, more passionate embrace.

It was Phoenix who pulled away first.

'I love you so much it hurts,' he told me, swinging his legs over the side of the bed and sitting hunched forward. 'It hurts that we have so little time together, that I don't have free will.'

'Is Hunter looking over your shoulder?' I asked, sitting beside him.

'Always.'

'He did that Marie thing again,' I told Phoenix, taking his hand and putting my small palm against his broad one. 'Earlier this evening – he made me look at an old blood stain on the floor. He trusted me with his own story.'

'Because you remind him of his wife.' Phoenix understood immediately. 'Three or four generations down the line, and he sees Marie in you.'

'He says it's my eyes.' Remembering the intensity of the

conversation made me shaky all over again. 'Hunter scares me, Phoenix. But there's one small corner of me that feels sorry for him.'

Phoenix smiled. 'He doesn't need your pity, believe me.'

'Maybe I'll check out his story one day. When I have some time – after we've solved Arizona's mystery.' And the Beautiful Dead went away from the far side to rest up and regenerate. 'The Peter Mentone murder case must be recorded in some old newspaper somewhere. I could look at files in the library, or in the newspaper office. They keep stuff like that, don't they?'

'I guess they do.' Right now Phoenix wasn't too interested in details of Hunter's history, so he steered us back to the present. 'When Arizona finally showed you her death mark, what did you think?'

'I was shocked.' She'd raised her thick hair and showed me the small angel wings – an act that seemed to put her whole fate into my hands once and for all. 'I'm thinking – was it an accident after all?'

'Not even a suicide?'

'It's possible. The shores of Hartmann are pretty rough and rocky. Maybe she slipped and fell.'

'But why was she out there at all?' Phoenix turned my hand so that it was resting in his. As he spoke, he traced the lines on my palm with his forefinger – the heart line crossing the life line. 'Arizona's not the hiking type, but there was no car at the scene, remember.'

'So someone drove her out there? And even if it was an accident – Arizona falling and hitting her head against a rock – how come this other person didn't dive in to save her?'

'Sure. And why didn't they call for help? You know it was a pair of hikers passing by who saw her body floating in the lake.'

I sat for a while without speaking. 'OK, try this,' I said at last. 'Arizona goes to see Kyle at Mike's Motors in this crazy, desperate mood. She uses the excuse of getting her car fixed. He's scared she's going to say too much in front of Mike Hamill, so he fixes to drive her out to Hartmann later that morning. The lake is way out of town – no one will see them there.'

Phoenix picked up the story. 'They meet and it all falls apart. Arizona loses control and threatens Kyle. She swears she'll stop him marrying Sable. We know he has a brutal temper – he strikes out, she stumbles, falls and hits her head so hard she breaks her neck.'

This was making a lot of sense.

'Kyle's scared,' I went on. 'He doesn't know if Arizona is alive or dead, but he realizes he's facing the biggest problem of his life – how to explain what happened to Arizona. The water's deep, he believes it's the only way to solve his problem. So he lifts Arizona from the rock and tosses her into the lake.'

Every detail seemed to slot into place now that we'd spoken it out loud. We totally convinced ourselves.

Phoenix nodded. 'Then Kyle leaves. He doesn't need an alibi – not many people know his connection with the dead girl. He acts stunned like everyone else when the body is eventually discovered. Later, the inquest hears Arizona was a loner, she was depressed. They give a verdict of suicide. No loose ends, no argument from the shell-shocked family. All neat and wrapped up.'

'And the whole town is stunned because it's the second death in weeks. First Jonas, then Arizona. I remember – that's when people start to believe there was a curse hanging over the kids of Ellerton. No one's thinking clearly. We're all afraid.'

'Kyle walks away.' Phoenix put the final piece in place.

'That's what he believes,' I added. 'But he doesn't know about the Beautiful Dead.'

We sat together admiring our polished version of events. It made me more determined than ever to force the truth out of Kyle Keppler. 'How long before dawn?' I asked Phoenix. 'How much time do we have before we set out for Forest Lake?'

He looked out at the stars and moon. 'Enough time for you to sleep,' he answered. 'I'll keep watch. You rest now.'

Amazingly I slept. Phoenix held my hand and didn't let go until I woke at first light, when the sun rose, hot red and gold, over the eastern mountains. I opened my eyes and the first thing I saw was the warm light glowing on his wonderful face.

'It's today or never,' he reminded me, as if I needed it.

We left the house like two thieves, climbing out of the upstairs window and jumping into my car. I let it freewheel down the drive, not turning the key in the ignition until we were clear of the house and heading for Centennial and the freeway beyond.

'Forget Peak Road – take the back track to Forest Lake,' Phoenix suggested. 'It cuts a couple of miles off our journey.'

'Yessir!' I tingled with the excitement of the lonely streets and the fact that it was our final shot at solving things for Arizona. For once, because I had Phoenix sitting by my side, the idea of Kyle Keppler didn't scare me. 'We need to get to Forest Lake before Kyle leaves for work.'

'And this time we don't care if Sable sees you,' Phoenix decided. 'We put all possible pressure on the guy to make him confess.'

'You'll be there?' I checked.

'Every step of the way. Now step on the gas. Drive, Darina, drive!'

We drove through dark mountains backed by a red-gold light, along a dirt track raising a cloud of dust, and no other car in sight.

Phoenix sat beside me wearing dark glasses, the round neckline of his white T-shirt making a strong contrast to the V of his half-unzipped leather jacket. I turned on the radio and listened to a country western song about saying a final goodbye to the one you love. Cruel death comes and takes the girl. 'Say goodbye, Marianna's leaving, Say goodbye, Marianna's gone.' The words 'leaving' and 'gone', repeated so many times in the chorus, tugged at my heart.

Then we came to Forest Lake, the hick town trying to live off its history and barely crawling into the twenty-first century.

Small wooden houses lined the roadside, beaten-up cars and trucks parked alongside. Shutters still closed, deer had strayed out of the forest and grazed the shabby, sloping lawns. The only light in town glowed under the awning of the diner where I'd drunk my cup of coffee and watched the stray brown-and-white dog.

'We're headed for White Eagle Road,' I told Phoenix, growing tense and gripping the steering wheel. I tried not to think too far ahead in case I lost my nerve.

'Watch out – you jumped a red light!' he warned.

I never even saw it, to tell the truth. We were on the right street now, looking for Keppler's red truck parked outside number 505.

'I think this is it.' I pointed to the house with the rough wire fence and overgrown yard. But there was no truck, no dogs, no sign of life.

'No one's home.' Phoenix studied the run-down house. 'How does that work? Where are Sable and the baby?'

'Wait here. Let me go and knock at the door,' I told him, my stomach churning as I walked up the drive. I was looking for and not seeing the baby stroller, maybe laundry hanging out to dry. My knuckles rapped at the glass panel in the door, rousing a dog in the yard next door. But no one appeared from inside number 505.

The neighbour's Labrador scrabbled his claws against the wooden fence. He jumped up so that his blunt black face appeared, jaws snapping.

'Jesus, Troy, quit that noise!' a voice said and a nosy-looking woman appeared at the fence. 'What do you want?' she asked me, no more friendly than her dog.

'I came to see Kyle,' I told her. 'This is his house, right?'

'Not home,' the woman grunted. 'Work it out – it's not rocket science.'

'So where did they go?'

The Kepplers' neighbour walked down to the end of her driveway and waited there for me to join her. 'Who's he – your boyfriend?' she asked, casting a glance towards Phoenix who sat with his collar up and his head turned away.

I nodded. 'Kyle and Sable – where did they go?'

'Who cares?' The woman was cagey, her dog still snarling in the back yard. 'The longer they stay away, the better I'll like it. Maybe then I'll get some peace.'

I tried hard to look sympathetic. 'Party animals, huh?'

'Drinkers,' she complained. 'Too much alcohol, and with a small kid to look after. It's not right.'

'They make a lot of noise?'

'Yelling all the time.' The skinny, bleached-blonde woman raised her eyes to heaven. 'The dogs bark, the kid cries all night long. Last night it was bad as it's ever been . . . Quit it, Troy, I'm trying to have a conversation!'

The chunky Labrador took no notice. I soldiered on against a background of high-volume barking. 'So – last night?' I prompted.

'Kyle gets home late, smashed out of his head like always. Her brother shows up with him, too drunk to ride a straight line.'

'Jon Jackson?'

'That's the one. They're drinking buddies, and God knows what else.'

I could have told her exactly the reason they showed up drunk last night – their route out of Foxton would have taken them past at least three bars. One beer to numb the pains in their guts and heads, another to settle the crazy thoughts about ghosts and corpses. But it would take more than two to get over what Hunter, Phoenix and Iceman had inflicted on them. They would have stayed for a third and a fourth.

'I'm on my back porch with the dog, so I hear everything.' The woman was offloading big time. She didn't look like she'd slept much and I guessed she was glad to find someone who would listen. 'Kyle falls over whatever crap is in the yard. He swears, the dogs yowl, the kid wakes up and starts to cry. Sable has had a bellyful, and she's no shrinking violet, believe me. She gives him a hard time. Her brother weighs in on Kyle's side. Soon there's World War Three going on twenty metres from where I'm sitting.'

'I hope no one got hurt,' I cut in.

The woman shrugged. She made it plain that actual domestic violence didn't come high on her scale of anti-social activity. 'It's the noise I can't take,' she sighed. 'Sable's yelling that it's the last time this is going to happen. She's packing her bag and taking the baby to her mom's place.'

'Which she did?'

The woman's smile showed a gap between her two front teeth. 'In Kyle's truck. That really stuck in his craw. Sable's out of there for good and he's yelling down the street for her to bring back his truck, his dogs and his baby or he'll kill her. What a joke. This is way past midnight, did I tell you?'

'Sounds like Sable had taken enough B.S. What did the guys do after she left?'

'What do you think? They drink a couple more cans. I set Troy on them, I'm so pissed. But Kyle kicks out at my dog and I hear Jon say he's getting the shotgun from inside the house. They laugh in my face when I go round to fetch Troy.'

'Did Jon bring the gun?'

The neighbour frowned. 'I didn't wait for it to happen. I grabbed my dog and pulled him back into my yard. I heard more cussing and then the sound of their bikes. I looked out of my window to see them ride off down the street – end of story.'

* * *

Phoenix and I drove back to Ellerton real fast. We reached Mike's Motors by 9.30 a.m., looking out this time for Kyle's black-and-chrome Dyna rather than his red truck.

'Boy, Kyle's brain must be hammering its way out of his skull!' Phoenix muttered as I parked by the concrete ramp leading up to the workshop.

'Yeah, plus his wife just left him, remember. I'm not looking for any positive attitude here.'

'*If* he showed up at work.'

We looked around – there was no Harley parked nearby. 'OK, so I go in and find out,' I decided.

This time Phoenix didn't let me go alone. Instead, he focused on his disappearing act, creating the glittering halo around his whole body, then gradually fading into invisibility. 'I'm right at your side,' he promised.

It was so weird, to hear his voice and the sound of his footsteps walking up the ramp with me, but to be able to see right through him.

'Hey,' I said to an older guy bent over the engine of a blue Toyota. 'We're . . . *I'm* looking for Kyle Keppler.

'That makes two of us.' Mike Hamill eased out from under the hood, then stood up straight. 'If you see him before I do, you can warn him he doesn't have a job to come back to.'

I gasped, coughing as I breathed in the smell of diesel and engine oil. 'You laid him off? Since when?'

'Since eight o'clock this morning when he didn't show up for work.' Hamill's voice was flat, giving the impression that Kyle had overstepped the mark once too often. 'He had his chances, but this time he blew it.'

'He has a family,' I pointed out. 'What happens to them if he doesn't get his job back?'

Mike Hamill lifted a dirty rag from a nearby oil drum and wiped his hands. He wore a long, dark moustache which made him look old and didn't match his greyer hair and eyebrows. His jeans were loose and stained, his plaid shirt straining across a sagging belly. 'Listen,' he told me, 'this isn't your business, but Kyle's family is the reason I kept him in work so long. My wife is best buddies with Sable's mom – the two of them put pressure on me to keep him in employment, yakk-yakk-yakk – you know how women do. Plus, when he's sober he knows his way around a car engine.'

'So does anyone know where he is right now?' Time was ticking by – Kyle's no-show was another serious setback.

'Sleeping his way through the mother of all hangovers, I reckon.' Mike lifted his cap and rubbed his forehead with the back of his hand. 'The story goes his drinking got out of hand again last night – my wife heard Sable finally packed her bag and left.'

I put on a pretty good act. 'My God, that's awful. His whole life is falling apart!'

'A guy who drinks and plays around like that – it's going to happen.' Mike went through into a tiny office and sat down on a revolving chair. He picked up the phone ready to dial.

'When you say, "plays around", you mean other women – *plural*?' This time I was truly shocked – no acting necessary.

'At least half a dozen,' he told me, his eyes starting to narrow as he wondered how come I was so interested in his ex-employee. 'Listen, honey, if you're Kyle's current squeeze, you should know that you're the latest in a long line. Over the years, Keppler has played pretty much the entire Ellerton field.'

'I'm not his latest . . . whatever!' *Let's get that straight!* I took a deep breath then pushed for more information. 'So he played around even after he got together with Sable?'

Mike made a sucking noise through his teeth. 'A wife and baby doesn't change a guy like Kyle, but you try telling Sable that. Karen – my wife – did warn her he was cheating on her – a year, eighteen months back.'

His stubby finger tapped numbers on the phone

keypad. I only had time to squeeze in one last question.

'Would that be when Kyle was in a relationship with Arizona Taylor?'

Mike's finger didn't complete the dial. He looked at me from under suspicious brows. 'The kid who drowned herself?'

I nodded.

'Yeah, around that time,' he said slowly.

'She was my friend.'

Mike made a sucking noise through his teeth. 'Well, I felt bad for her – she was way too young. You or someone else who cared about her should have told her Kyle was bad news.'

'I didn't know she was involved until it was too late.'

He flicked back eighteen months, remembering Arizona. 'Poor kid, she could have done a whole lot better than Kyle Keppler. I remember the times she would hang out here, trying to act tough. She wasn't – not really.'

'Did she come to the workshop the day she drowned in the lake?'

Mike's dialling finger got ready again. 'She came a lot of days, and yeah, she did call that morning. She lost control a little when she found out Kyle wasn't here – he was nursing his usual sore head, I guess.'

'He missed work?' I needed to be doubly sure.

'Yeah. Lucky I wasn't busy that day. Later, we all heard the news about the girl – Arizona.'

'Thanks,' I said, letting air out of my lungs in a long sigh.

'This isn't stuff you wanted to hear – right?' Mike Hamill was a decent guy and he picked up on my obvious disappointment. But he did get it totally wrong when he dumped me and Arizona in the same cheated-on category. 'Kyle's a good-looking guy and he can get whichever girl he wants, but you need to break off whatever it is you have going with him.'

'I don't—'

'Honestly, honey, he's not worth it. You can't trust the guy even to give you the time of day.'

The fact was, we'd got to 10.00 a.m. on our final day and we were no nearer to tracking Kyle down. I turned in the direction I thought Phoenix might be and told him we were getting nowhere.

He spoke from way in front. 'We learned a lot from Mike Hamill,' he pointed out. 'For starters, we know now that Arizona and Kyle didn't arrange to meet at Hartmann.'

'So we're worse than nowhere,' I groaned. 'We only had the one theory and now that's blown apart.'

A guy passing by caught me apparently talking to

myself as I got in my car. He gave me an odd look then pulled out his cell phone.

Hearing Phoenix sink into the leather passenger seat, I quickly drove off. 'I wish I didn't know that Kyle is a serial cheat.'

'Yeah, it sucks.'

We both thought about what the news would do to Arizona. 'Do we need to tell her?' I asked.

'That's a hard one to call. I don't think we do, unless it's part of the final picture.'

'Which we're no nearer to finding out.' Frustration was gnawing at me as I drove aimlessly towards the centre of town. 'Keppler could be anywhere. How do we corner him if we don't know where he is?'

I stopped at a red light for pedestrians to use the crossing. Among them was a young woman pushing a stroller. It took me a couple of seconds to recognize her as Sable Keppler with her baby!

'Pull over,' Phoenix said, after going through the same delayed reaction.

I turned into a gas station and we watched Sable meet up with a woman who looked like an older version of herself – the same dark hair and definite jawline. Small and slight, they were both dressed in tight jeans and loose jackets which drew attention to their thin-as-sticks legs, with striped scarves wound around their necks. They bunched together on the sidewalk, deep in conversation.

'I want to hear what they're saying.' Deciding to risk leaving the car, I crossed the road, as if I wanted to browse in a store window. A creak of leather and the faint sound of footsteps told me that Phoenix had come too.

The store sold fishing rods, which was as fascinating as you can get. I tried to look interested in the reels, floats and flies.

'I bought diapers.' The woman who I guessed was Sable's mother held up a plastic carrier bag. 'What else do we need?'

'I left Mischa's feeding cup and bowl back at the house – her favourites.' Sable made a list. 'Plus I need baby wipes and comforters.'

'OK, so we call at the pharmacy on the way home. We can pick everything up there. Did Kyle try to call?'

'Five or six times. I let it ring out.'

'You'll have to talk to him sooner or later.' Sable's mother took the stroller and started to push it towards a parking lot. The baby strained at the straps, turning to see whether Sable was following.

'Not today,' Sable insisted, taking her phone from her pocket and turning it off.

I waited for them to move on a few paces then I

started to follow. It felt very bad to be witnessing the wreckage of Kyle's family – until now his wife and baby hadn't seemed real. But here Sable was, her face pinched by the cold wind, her mouth set in a downwards curve. And the kid had a name – Mischa. She was a pretty baby with dark curls.

'Listen, Sable – I called your brother,' Sable's mom admitted as they reached her car.

'You shouldn't have done that.' Sable was angry. She lifted Mischa out of the stroller and strapped her into the car seat, folding the stroller with too much force before she threw it into the trunk.

'I was worried about him.' The older woman held open the driver's door, trying to justify her action. 'If he was out-of-his-head drunk, like you said, he could have crashed his bike, ridden off the road – anything.'

'You think I care?' Sable leaned in to check the straps on Mischa's seat. 'Jon and Kyle – they're the same.'

'But Sable – you're Jon's sister and he loves you. He wanted to talk things through with you. I said for him to come to town.'

'You told him where to find us?' Sable walked away from the car then stormed back again. 'Listen to me, Mom, I don't want to talk to Jon – not now, and not ever. He may be my brother, but he's a loser, OK!'

'Baby, listen—'

'No, you listen. You want to see your son? Fine – you stay here and talk to him. But you give me the car key and let me drive.' Sable snatched the key and got in the car.

Her mother tried to lean in through the window. 'Where will I find you?'

Sable took a deep breath and tried to calm herself. 'Mischa's tired. I'm going to take her back to your place and put her to bed. Where else do I go?'

And what else could Phoenix and I do now except follow Sable? We ran to my car and hit the road in time to see her swing off from the main street down a road leading to the highway. Here, on Daler Street, the houses were set back from the road and spaced apart, a little bigger and neater than the ones on White Eagle Road. Some were painted in pastel shades of yellow and blue, with white porches and flowers growing in the yard. Sable turned into the drive of a grey gabled house that needed work.

I pulled on to the sidewalk, watching Sable take the baby out of the car, hearing dogs bark from inside the house. 'This is a total mess,' I sighed.

Next to me Phoenix materialized in a halo of light. He looked tense and unsure. 'It's complicated,' he agreed.

'These people – Sable and Mischa – they don't deserve to have their lives torn apart.'

'By us.' I looked ahead and saw what would happen to this family if we proved Kyle had killed Arizona. Then I turned it around. 'Hey, they're doing a good job of tearing their own lives apart.'

'And we need justice for Arizona.' Phoenix too was able to refocus. 'So we go ahead?'

I nodded. 'We find out who drove Arizona out to Hartmann and why.'

The way it worked was – Jon Jackson found his mother in town soon after Sable had driven off with Mischa and it didn't take long for him to learn where his sister was. Five minutes after she arrived at their mom's house, Jon showed up on his sleek black Softtail.

Phoenix and I were still in my car, talking tactics.

We saw Jon ride right up to the front door and heard him yell Sable's name. When he didn't get an answer, he stormed into the house. Seconds later, he, Sable and two German shepherds burst on to the front porch.

My car wasn't parked close enough for me to hear what the brother and sister were saying, so I relied on Phoenix.

'She says she doesn't want to talk to him,' he reported. 'She's telling him to get the hell out.'

I watched Sable eyeball her tall, scary brother. He was dark, like her, with heavy eyebrows and a scowling mouth. She only came up to his chest, which she poked with her fingers every word she spoke.

'She's telling him she and Kyle are all washed up. He's saying for her to give the guy another chance. There's a lot of cussing on both sides.'

'Shall I drive nearer to the house?'

'A little. Now Jon's telling her he's on her side – more than she'll ever know.'

'What does that mean?' I could see this was an intense relationship between brother and sister, and now, as I crept closer I could listen in for myself.

'Kyle did some stuff – we know that,' Jon insisted. 'But he learned his lesson.'

Sable gave a hollow laugh. 'So last night – you call that learning a lesson?'

'We rode out to Foxton with a bunch of guys,' Jon tried to explain. 'Do you believe in ghosts, Sable? No, me neither until I saw what went on up on that ridge. You heard the rumours about the kids who died coming back to haunt the place? They're all true.'

'That's the liquor talking!' she scoffed, and she shoved him down from the porch. 'Well, you and Kyle – both of you – can mess with your own heads and fantasize about ghosts all you like. You leave now, Jon, and you tell Kyle not to come calling.'

Too late – there'd already been communication between Jon and Kyle, who roared on to Daler Street on his Dyna just as Sable said her 'liquor talking' line.

That left me skewered where I was on my cream leather car seat and Phoenix hastily performing his vanishing act again.

Of course Kyle Keppler saw me and wrenched open my door. He didn't yell – he just threw me a look of total hate and told me calmly to get out of my car, which I found scarier than the expected physical violence.

The dogs ran snarling to the fence. By the front door, Sable began to pound her fists against her brother's chest.

I stood on the rough grass and gravel verge, quaking in my shoes.

'What's the deal?' Kyle asked, taking my wrist and walking me down the road.

Behind us, I could hear Phoenix's footsteps brushing through the dry grass.

Our feet crunched on the stones. 'Are you planning to tell my wife about me and the dead girl? Because, if you open your mouth and say the name, you're dead yourself.'

'Why would I tell?' I used all my strength to try and

break his grip – the skin on my wrist burned with the effort. 'Arizona's gone. Nothing's going to change that.'

'So quit poking your nose where it's not wanted.' Finally he let me break loose. 'You're about to turn around and get back in your car. I'm about to tell Sable I'm sorry and get on with my life.'

The arrogance of the guy angered me. 'It'll take a whole lot more than sorry,' I told him. 'Besides, you lost your job. Mike Hamill said to let you know.'

A couple of nerves flicked in Keppler's jaw. He closed his eyes and tilted his head back. In another second I reckon he would have lashed out at me with that massive fist.

But along came Jon Jackson, toting a shotgun. He aimed it straight at me.

I stared down that long barrel and calmly thought, *So this is what it's like*. My last moments, stretching out in slow motion, yellow grass rustling by the roadside, a plane leaving a white trail in the cornflower-blue sky.

When Phoenix, Hunter and Arizona suddenly materialized, I thought, *So . . . not now, not like this*.

Hunter walked between me and Jackson. He grasped the barrel of the gun and tilted it to an angle of forty-five degrees.

Jackson and Kyle lunged at Hunter but Phoenix felled

them both. They sprawled in the dry grass, the shotgun sliding out of reach.

I glanced at Arizona. There was disappointment in her eyes as deep as the ocean as she gazed at her lover lying in the dirt.

'I can't get through to him,' I muttered. 'I tried, you have to believe me.'

'So Keppler takes the hard route. He gets to time travel,' Hunter said sternly. 'Don't feel we reached the end of the line, Arizona. There's one more thing we can do.'

11

It hurts like hell when you travel through time – much more than the zombie mind-zap they use to wipe your memory clean.

An overpowering energy forces its way inside you and twists every muscle and sinew. The pain concentrates between your shoulder blades, burning and tearing until you turn around and you see you have beautiful angel wings which you can spread wide and feel the wind rustle through the pure white feathers.

It was Hunter, me, Arizona, Kyle and Jon Jackson, all journeying back exactly one year plus seven days to replay the truth behind the mystery of Arizona's death.

You would say that we flew through the stormy air, except that there's a whirling force carrying you back, a kind of time tunnel that sucks you in so that your wings don't function until you come out the other end and you're back at the critical moment, by Hartmann Lake, hovering above the ground and watching the action.

Hartmann in the fall – our last-ditch, last-minute attack on the truth. Frost lies on the ground though it's after midday. A layer of thin ice has formed at the water's edge.

And the water – it's dazzlingly clear and smooth, a bottomless greenish-blue. On the far shore, a slope covered in golden aspens rises to rocky scree. It could be in a travel brochure, I know. *Visit the unspoiled Rocky Mountains. See Nature in all its glory.*

And how powerful is Hunter now, holding us all in that time warp, making us bear witness.

We see Kyle's red truck parked under some redwoods, two figures standing beside it. And of course, the figures are Kyle and Arizona a year ago – she's still alive. It's how Phoenix and I pictured it.

'This is the last time,' Kyle tells her. 'I'm about to marry my girlfriend, so we have this one final conversation, period.'

Arizona is suffering. Her eyes are too dark, her face too pale.

'You hear me?' Kyle grabs her arm and pulls her away from the truck. 'You don't call me, you don't come round to Mike's any more – understand?'

'Who told you?' Her small voice belongs to someone

else, not to the gutsy, proud Arizona I knew.

'I just know – OK!'

Amongst the group of invisible observers, angel-wing Kyle and Jon panicked and made a bid for freedom. They turned towards the lake, attempting to fly off. Hunter shook his head. He used a storm of invisible wings to hold them back.

'So is that why you called me – to bring me out here and tell me you don't want to see me again?' It's pre-zombie Arizona pleading one last time. 'I don't believe you, Kyle. You've tried it before but I know you can't let me go!'

Zoom back out to my vantage point and what do you see? Two small figures and a red truck in an empty wilderness, autumn frost in the trees, a guy about to lose control.

'You'd better believe me, Arizona. I'm marrying Sable. You and me – we had some fun, but it's over.'

Arizona-alive reacts like he's slapped her in the face. 'Fun?' She's unable to make sense of the word. 'Is that what this has been to you? What about the personal stuff you told me – about you as a lonely, lost kid spending whole days out here by the lake alone, not fitting in, hating your family, needing to cut loose?'

Kyle shrugs. 'It was true.'

'So where did that guy I loved go? Where did this one I don't understand come from?' She makes an attempt to put her arms around his neck but he pushes her away.

'Everything changed,' he mutters. 'We have to move on.'

'And what if I say no? What happens if I talk to – to Sable?'

Beside me, angel-wing Arizona covered her face in shame.

That's it – Kyle loses control. 'You try it, Arizona, and you're dead.'

'Dead' falls like a pebble into water, ripples widening.

'You can't stop me,' she protests. 'I'm a person. I have rights, just like anybody else – you can't push me back into a closet like I never existed.'

He's cruel – totally cruel. 'You never did exist for me – not really,' he tells her with a sneer. 'Beside someone real like Sable who talks my language, you're nothing – a spoiled kid who cries to get her own way. When did you ever have to lift a finger to get what you wanted?'

'You think that?' At last she fights back. 'You imagine I click my fingers and people come running? That's how much you know me!'

'Screwed-up little rich kid, so far up yourself it's not

true.' He pushes her away from the truck, out from under the shadowy redwoods. Now they're standing on a rocky ledge overhanging the lake. 'Wait till you see who I brought with me, then you'll know I'm serious.'

Another storm of wings told me that Kyle and Jon were fighting Hunter again and failing to flee. He held them right where they were, forcing them to look down on the year-ago action.

'We're alone out here,' Arizona cries, looking wildly around. 'What do you mean – you brought someone with you?'

'OK, Jon,' Kyle says, keeping all expression out of his voice. 'It's time.'

And Jon Jackson, dressed in black T-shirt and jeans, steps out from behind a rock. He's not alone. He has Raven with him.

Arizona's bewildered brother has no clue where he is or why he's here. He's terrified. Arizona-alive is stunned into silence. Beautiful Dead Arizona covers her mouth with her hand. Terrified, as in small-animal petrified when a predator puts out a paw and taps the victim before it unsheathes its claws.

Raven cowers helplessly by Jackson's side.

'Easy, huh?' Jon Jackson gloats. 'I found him by the lake at the school – there was no one else around. I got him in my truck real easy – he's doesn't weigh more than sixty pounds.'

Arizona makes a run towards her brother. She only goes a few steps before Kyle gets in her way. She stumbles and slips towards the edge of the ledge.

Raven sees her and makes his own charge towards her, which Jackson intercepts.

'I trusted you – why did I ever do that?' Arizona is bent double with shock, fear and disbelief. Kyle stands over her. 'I never in my whole life told anyone about Raven except for you. Kyle, don't do this to him. Let him go.'

Raven struggles with Jackson. He's weak and uncoordinated, his arms and legs uncontrolled. I never saw anything so sad – ever.

'Let him go!' Arizona screams.

Her panic gets to Raven. He flails his puny arms against Jackson's chest. For a second I think he can escape. Then Jackson spins him around and pins his arms behind his back, lifting him off his feet before he dumps him on the ground against a tree.

Kyle seems unhappy with this descent into violence. He turns his back and takes a step away.

So it's Jackson who ramps up the threats. 'You go within a mile of my sister and this happens again,' he warns Arizona, jerking his thumb towards Raven and walking right up to her. 'I can snatch the kid from that school whenever I like, do whatever I want to him – you hear me?'

'I said to let him go,' Arizona begs.

Raven has brought his knees up to his chest and is rocking himself to and fro.

Jackson stands between Arizona and her brother. 'Not until you swear to back off from Kyle and my sister.'

She shakes her head desperately. 'Was this your idea?' she says to Keppler, who still has his back to them.

'Don't blame him. Snatching the kid was down to me,' Jackson boasts. 'And I'll hurt him if I have to – you'd better believe it.'

Raven is sobbing. Arizona succeeds in pushing past Jackson and goes down on her knees. She puts her arms around her brother. 'It's OK, buddy,' she whispers. 'Everything is going to be OK.'

Which it wasn't and never would be, and my heart practically stopped as I witnessed this with angel-wing Hunter, Arizona, Kyle and Jackson.

Beautiful Dead Arizona moved in close to confront her ex-boyfriend. 'Were you crazy? Had you any idea what kidnapping my brother would do to him?'

Kyle couldn't look her in the eye. 'You wouldn't listen to me,' he muttered. 'Jon and me – we had to think of something to make you stay quiet.'

'You and half a dozen other girls,' Jackson sneered. 'Yeah, Arizona – you were not alone!'

He might as well have stabbed her in the heart. In that one statement he killed the ragged remains of her dreams.

'Is that true?' she asked angel-wing Kyle in that pleading, little-girl voice.

But year-ago stuff is happening by the lake again. Raven has broken free from his sister, jumped to his feet and starts to run. This time he makes it off the rocky ledge and back in amongst the tall pines. He vanishes in the shadows. Kyle is closest, so he sets off after him.

Arizona calls out. 'Raven, don't run. Stay with me!'

As she tries to follow her brother, Jon Jackson gets rough with her. Arizona shoves him to one side with all her strength. He's off-balance. It looks like he will slide towards the lake.

But he grabs an aspen sapling and puts the brake on. He finds a foothold and springs back up to the ledge, lunging at Arizona as she tries to kick him back down. She's using her feet, lashing out, totally crazy. It's not a fair contest – Jackson is almost twice as big and strong.

He lunges and forces her back against the trunk of the redwood where Raven had crouched in his misery. You can almost hear the breath forced out of her as he smashes her against the rough surface. She puts up both arms to fend him off. But he soon gets his hands around her neck, wrenching at her like a rag doll and beating her back against the tree – once, twice, three times. She stops struggling. He lets her go and she slides to the ground.

Arizona lies there for about five seconds, a lifetime. Jackson hesitates. He bends over her as if he's looking for signs of life, and when he doesn't find any he takes a step back. He looks over his shoulder, wondering where Kyle and Raven ended up. There's no sign of either of them. He prods Arizona's body with his foot. She doesn't respond.

She lies on her back on the granite rock, her head at an angle, her arms flung wide.

And then, in a way that a hunter would heave a shot deer on to his shoulders, Jackson lifts Arizona and carries her to the very edge of the rock. He tilts forward and lets her body slip, not quite clear of the ledge, so that it thuds against the rock on its descent. Thud – and then splash into the lake.

Maybe contact with the cold water revives her. For a few moments Arizona comes back to life, strikes out with her arms and struggles towards the shore. She doesn't give in to death without a fight.

Jackson's in the water now – he leaps from the ledge and straight away he catches hold of Arizona. He easily overpowers her and drags her away from the shallows, seeming to rise out of the water like a black sea creature, his hair slicked back and flattened against his skull, his hands around Arizona's throat. He forces her face under the water, he holds her there until there's no life left in her body. He holds her under until she's dead.

Then the dark creature wades towards the shore. Further out in the lake Arizona's body rises to the surface – arms wide, long hair like waterweeds fanning out from her white face. Her blank eyes stare at the sky.

We were wrong. We were all wrong, all the way down the line. Arizona didn't kill herself and neither did Kyle Keppler. Hunter the overlord held the guilty man at the scene of his crime using the sheer strength of his willpower. He gave us all what seemed like an age to stare at Jon Jackson.

Kyle broke the silence. 'You told me it was an accident.'

Jackson shook his head. 'You believed what you wanted to believe.'

'You told me straight – Arizona fell and hit her head.'

'What do you care? Your problem went away, end of story.' If Jackson felt sorry for what he did, he hid it well. 'I got you out of there without anyone seeing us, didn't I? I was the one who kept his head.'

I was still gazing at Arizona's floating corpse, the

glittering surface and the dead stare.

Beautiful Dead Arizona was beside me. We saw year-ago Kyle emerge from the trees with Raven, watched his shocked reaction as he spotted the body in the lake.

'You killed her,' angel-wing Kyle said in that emotionless voice.

'Get ready to leave,' Hunter told us all. 'We've seen all we need to see.'

12

We travelled faster than you can believe, blasted by a wind, buoyed up by a million wings. We twisted through a time tunnel, felt the empty gaze of countless skulls whirling over us in the darkness. Arizona was the one who led the way back to the present, and the scrubland at the edge of Daler Street.

'What's the deal?' Kyle asked, taking my wrist and walking me down the road. 'Are you planning to tell my wife about me and the dead girl? Because, if you open your mouth and say the name, you're dead yourself.'

'Why would I tell?' I used all my strength to try and break his grip – the skin on my wrist burned with the effort. 'Arizona's gone. Nothing's going to change that.'

'So quit poking your nose where it's not wanted.' Finally he let me break loose. 'You're about to turn around and get back in your car. I'm about to tell Sable I'm sorry and get on with my life.'

The arrogance of the guy angered me. 'It'll take a whole lot more than sorry,' I told him. 'Besides, you lost your job. Mike Hamill said to let you know.'

A couple of nerves flicked in Keppler's jaw. He closed his eyes and tilted his head back. In another second I reckon he would have lashed out at me with that massive fist.

But along came Jon Jackson, toting a shotgun. He aimed it straight at me. I stared down that long barrel and calmly thought, So this is what it's like. My last moments, stretching out in slow motion, yellow grass rustling by the roadside, a plane leaving a white trail in the cornflower-blue sky.

Knowing now what his brother-in-law had done out at Hartmann, Kyle strode between me and Jackson. He grasped the gun and wrenched it from his hands, turned it on his brother-in-law and pressed the barrel against his chest.

'Kyle, don't – I don't believe you!' Jackson gasped. But he was scared – you could see the fear, and smell it like they say you can.

Keppler backed him down the road, the gun at his chest. Hunter kept me and Arizona fixed to the spot.

'Kyle, you saw how Arizona acted – she was like a wild thing. What else could I do?'

It's a terrible thing to hear a guy plead for his life and

to feel no sympathy. I so wanted Kyle to pull that trigger, I admit.

'You said she drowned.' Kyle wasn't listening to Jackson. He still held the image of him battering Arizona against the tree, hauling her to the edge of the lake and throwing her in – thud and splash.

'It happened – I didn't plan it. We got the boy back into town and dumped him there without anyone seeing us, didn't we? We walked away.'

God knows how empty and hopeless it feels to have the lethal steel pressed to your heart, to have words pouring out of your mouth, knowing that they're a waste of your final breaths.

Kyle's back was turned to Hunter, Arizona and me. We didn't see his face as he squeezed the trigger and the sound brought people to their doors. It stopped the traffic which headed to and from the freeway.

In a way that gunshot ended it. In another way, it didn't.

Personally, I will never forget the car-stopping blast from the gun and the way it echoed up and down Daler Street. It lives on in my mind and the minds of everyone who heard it.

Jon Jackson staggered. His knees buckled and he fell on his back. Keppler threw the gun aside.

Anyone witnessing it from the outside would say the killer's next reaction was weird. They saw him bend double as if in pain, rock on his heels and twist in his effort to get away from the scene, though his legs wouldn't carry him and his features froze in an agonized mask. He spun and almost fell on to the dead man, but regained his balance just in time.

Only Arizona, Phoenix and I knew this was Hunter's work. We watched him wipe his victim's memory clean of the time-trip to Hartmann exactly one year plus seven days ago to the minute.

Now he would never know why he'd shot Jackson. How crazy is that?

The shrinks would describe it as unaccountable rage, perhaps fuelled by alcohol and a secret grudge against Jackson which Keppler refused to reveal. They might label him psychotic – unable to recognize the consequences of his actions – and offer him psychiatric treatment while they locked him up.

The sirens sounded. Arizona, Hunter, Phoenix and I still had our wings. We hovered above the houses, watching the cops establish a crime scene and drive Keppler away.

Hunter allowed Arizona one last visit to her beloved Raven.

He sent us – her and me – from Daler Street to the Taylors' *Mountain Living* home so that she could see for herself there was a way forward.

It was me knocking on the door of 2850 North 22 Street, minus my wings, with an invisible Arizona at my shoulder.

To my surprise, it was Peter Hall who let me into the house. 'How come you're back?' I asked.

'A miracle – Allyson had a change of heart.' With a wry grin, the old man led me across the vast lobby. 'Frank's here too. Plus, the Arizona photographs came out of storage.'

Sure enough, her incredibly photogenic face stared out from brushed silver frames. A large, life-size portrait hung over the stone fireplace.

During her last minutes on earth, my Beautiful Dead friend was breathing fast, treading silently beside me.

'So, will they still sell the house and move away?' I asked.

Which was when Allyson and Frank emerged from his music room. I'd like to say there was a transformation here too – that they were relaxed and happy, with warm smiles on their faces and a welcoming light in their eyes. But no – they both looked strained, drained, uncertain and mixed up.

Allyson picked up the thread. 'Everything is under discussion,' she told me. 'The house, our marriage – everything.'

At least they were talking. And for me this added up to another miracle.

'The focus has to be on Raven,' Allyson insisted. 'He's been through a lot. We feel we need to offer him more stability – stick to his routine, surround him by familiar objects.'

'And people,' Frank added. 'My wife tells me you paid him a visit. He seems to have formed an attachment.'

Allyson managed to smile. 'Quite literally,' she recalled. 'Raven grabbed a hold of Darina's jacket and no way could I get him to let go.'

'So we're glad for you to call by whenever you like.' Frank led the way through to the back of the house and a big expanse of wooded garden, which overlooked a cool, long distance view of Amos Peak.

I spotted Raven sitting in the shade of an aspen tree, his dark-blue jacket zippered tight under his chin. For a second I was anxious as I felt Arizona leave my side and head towards him.

Maybe she reached out and touched his face. I saw him raise his hand to his cheek and brush something away – once, twice, three times.

'Raven, Arizona's friend called by to see you,' Allyson told him.

He blinked and jerkily turned his head in my direction. It took him a while but then he slid me into a memory slot that seemed to make some sense. He got up and walked to me.

'Hey,' I said.

He blinked again. Slowly he put his hand in his pocket, pulled out a piece of neatly folded paper and handed it to me.

I unfolded it. *Look,* I wanted to tell Arizona – *it's the picture he drew of you!* I held the drawing in trembling hands.

Boy, did those aspen leaves quiver and shake – Arizona sighing as if her heart would break. But at least she knew that her parents weren't about to lock her brother up and throw away the key.

Then Raven led the way back into the house. He grabbed my hand and showed me the photographs of his sister restored to the shelves and tables. We stood a long time under the one that hung over the fireplace. It showed something unusual – Arizona smiling. Yes, really. Her hair was glossy, dark and perfect. She wore a silver choker necklace and big hooped earrings. And she was happy.

'Cool,' I told Raven.

They said his brain couldn't relate to facial expressions but I have an issue with that.

Standing there, gazing up at the portrait with Arizona standing invisible beside him, I say Raven totally knew what that smile meant, that it came from his sister's heart and would be there every time he walked through the lobby and looked up into her amazing, almond-shaped green eyes.

'You have your justice and your freedom,' Hunter told Arizona. 'No one promised it wouldn't taste bitter.'

He had given us a few moments back at Foxton before Arizona left for good.

The Beautiful Dead gathered inside the barn, seeming to need the safety and shelter of the shadowy building.

Eve and Donna stood close by her side. Summer held her hand. Standing with a silent Phoenix I felt sad and heart-sick for her.

Arizona hung her head. 'Back there at Hartmann I saw myself for what I really was – eaten up by jealousy, selfish, stupid . . .'

'A human being,' Hunter said without judging, walking out of the barn.

The door closed and I wondered when I would see him again.

'Hunter's right,' Summer said. 'We've all acted that way.'

'I put Raven's life at risk. I was so needy. I hate that.'

Don't! I thought. *Don't beat yourself up.*

Phoenix read my mind and gestured for the others to leave us alone. 'I won't be far away,' he whispered to me as he too left. Soon the barn was deserted except for me and Arizona. We stood in the cool shadows, me trying to slip in under the barrier of self-hatred that Arizona had built up again.

'I plan to visit Raven again – maybe tomorrow,' I told her quietly. 'I'll take some new Warhol pictures for him to look at.' It was the best way I knew to finally set her free.

Slowly she closed her eyes, took a deep breath and said the three simple words that meant everything to me. 'Thank you, Darina.'

'He knows me,' I insisted. 'You saw that he links me with you.'

'You're right,' she agreed. Her time was up. She was slipping away.

'I'll talk to him about you,' I promised. 'I can't be his shadow, like you wanted to be. But I'll keep on telling him how you loved him and always will. How you were a strong and crazy girl, how I got to understand and admire you in a way I never believed I would.'

Arizona stared deep into my eyes. 'Sorry, Darina. I gave you a hard time.'

'You did. Now I know why.'

'I never . . .' She searched for the right words. 'I never exactly got my balance right when I was alive. I was always, *always* teetering on the edge of that ledge, ready to fall.'

I nodded, no words necessary on my part. Anyway, she could read my mind.

'You know what that's like,' she noted, as a wind came into the barn and gently opened then shut the door. 'You know it leads you into making desperate choices.'

'Sometimes.'

'I mean Kyle,' she explained.

'But not Phoenix,' I argued, as he walked back in. I smiled at him. 'He happens to be the best choice I made in my whole life.'

'I want to second that,' he told me. And he grasped my hand like he would never let go.

Arizona sighed. 'Lucky you, Darina. And yet you lost him.'

Phoenix kept tight hold of me. It gave me strength. I

spoke to him, not Arizona. 'Then I found you again. Out here at Foxton, for twelve months.'

'A whole year,' he promised.

I stared into his pale-blue eyes, shimmering crystal clear like lake water. 'And soon I get to work with you to solve your mystery – to find out why you died.'

Phoenix lifted my hand to his pale, cold cheek. 'You'll set me free,' he sighed. Then he turned to include Arizona. 'Darina and I get to go with you to Hartmann,' he told Arizona.

We stood by the icy shore as the sun went down. Phoenix held my hand while we watched Arizona wade out into the water.

The lake stretched for ever, the trees on the far shore were lost in a grey mist.

She was waist-deep, her fingertips skimming the surface. She half turned to look at us.

Her long hair was black, her angel wings pure white.

'Go!' we whispered.

She turned and looked ahead. Hartmann was vast and silent.

Then the mist drifted in from the far shore. It shrouded Arizona and took her away.

Phoenix and I looked for her in the mist for a long

time, listened for any sound, standing hand in hand, knowing that she was gone from the far side.

'Let's go,' I told Phoenix at last.

Turn the page for a sneak peek of

BOOK 3 – SUMMER

BEAUTIFUL DEAD

Who decides what's normal and what's not?

People around here sigh and say, 'No one died in six months, thank God. Maybe the worst is over.'

I say, 'Wait, it's not finished, not by a long way.'

'No one else died. Now we can get our lives back on track.'

'Ride the bus into school, why don't you? Go to work, don't dwell on the past. Fine,' I think, but I keep my cynical mouth shut and put one foot in front of the other along with the rest of Ellerton.

Normal is grey and narrow. Normal is not daring to look back.

At night I dream in widescreen, high definition technicolour.

Phoenix is there, centre screen, full of life. He's coming right at me, smiling, reaching out his hand. I take it and his blue grey eyes shining out from under a sweep of dark hair are talking to me, telling me he loves me. When he rests his arm around my shoulder, I feel the warm weight of it. Awake, I'm alone. They try to get near me – Laura, Zoey, Logan and the rest. 'Look ahead, Darina. There's so much to live for.' Meaning, you're seventeen years old for chrissake, you only knew Phoenix Rohr for a couple of months. OK so you lost him in a street fight and that was tough but you have your whole life in front of you. Normal, grey stuff.

I push them away. I prefer my multi-colour dreams.

Phoenix and me cross-legged on a rock in the middle of Deer Creek. Silver flashes on the clear water, blood-red sun over Amos Peak. Phoenix's lips on mine, full and soft. I run my fingers from the nape of his neck down his spine. His skin is smooth, warm and tanned, there's no angel-wing death mark between his shoulder blades where the knife went in. It's like we've been together since the day we were born.

Awake again, I'm driving out of town. I'm cold, it's February and the grey voices are winning.

'I fixed up another session with Kim Reiss,' Laura just informed me. 'Please talk to her, Darina. It's bad for you to bottle up your emotions this way.'

I'm cold, pushing eighty miles per hour with the top

down. The way the wind flaps through my hair reminds me of beating wings. The mountains ahead look black.

What do I say to Kim the Shrink in her primrose-yellow room? I'm cold, I'm hurting, I haven't seen my Beautiful Dead boyfriend in twelve whole weeks.

Eighty-four days of driving out to Foxton since Arizona stepped into Hartmann Lake, her angel wings spread wide. It was late fall, before Christmas and a blank New Year. I stood next to you, Phoenix, at the lake's edge, while angel-wing Arizona walked up to her waist in the clear green water and a mist came to take her. 'Go,' we said.

You held my hand and your hand was cold as ice.

Foxton is where I'll find you and it won't be a dream. One cold day in the deep snow, when your overlord decides it's time, you'll be there at the barn door, waiting for me. Maybe today.

Black rocks rise sheer to either side, a grey strip of road threading through. The car engine purrs and the wind tears at me.

Today. I picture Phoenix at the barn door, back from the dead, here on the far side. The frozen chambers of my heart fire up. I'm in his arms and this time I will never let go.